The Last Warrior

SUZANNE PIERSON ELLISON

rising moon
Books for Young Readers from Northland Publishing

OTHER BOOKS FROM RISING MOON:

Walks in Beauty, by Hazel Krantz

Available in the spring of 1998:
Twilight Boy, by Tim Green

The cover illustration was rendered in acrylic on panel
The text type was set in Caslon 224
The display type was set in Copperplate
Composed and manufactured in the United States of America
Art directed by Rudy J. Ramos
Designed by Billie Jo Bishop
Edited by Stephanie Bucholz
Production Supervised by Lisa Brownfield

FIRST IMPRESSION
ISBN 0-87358-678-6 (hc)
ISBN 0-87358-679-4 (sc)
Library of Congress Catalog Card Number pending

Reprinted by arrangement with Northland Publishing Company.
Printed in the USA.
10 9 8 7 6 5 4 3 2 1

THIS NOVEL IS DEDICATED TO
my dear friend, Connie Bennett,
who kept the candle burning,
and to the wonderful students
of Balboa Middle School, who
inspire and humble me.

Solito's Homeland

ARIZONA

NEW MEXICO

Santa Fe

Flagstaff

Albuquerque

Fort Apache

Phoenix

Tucson

Fort Bowie

MEXICO

xxxxx Chiricahua Apache Territory

White Mountain Apache Territory

...... Other Western Apache Territory

- - - - State and International Borders

CHAPTER

1

Arizona Territory, Summer 1886

IT WAS TOO DARK above the gritty bluff for me to see the warriors, but I could hear their ponies snort and blow as they trotted to a stop. To the south, I knew, lay the ranch we would strike to gather desperately needed cattle for our starving people. We must also seize fresh horses.

My uncle leaned so close that our elbows touched before he whispered, "You must wait for us by the peeling red-bark trees. That-which-comes-dragging will never find you there."

I knew "that-which-comes-dragging" was the secret warriors' code for some everyday Apache word—bear, wolf, enemy?—but I could not recall which one. I nodded anyway. I was not about to let my uncle know that I had forgotten anything he had taught me. Even if I made no mistakes tonight, I would still need one more raid to complete my ritual training. Without it, I would never be considered a true Chiricahua Apache brave.

I wanted to tell Uncle Angry-He-Spears-Bluecoats that I'd keep the horses silent, but I couldn't remember the secret warriors' name for them. It was all I could do to keep track of the warpath taboos.

Gravely I promised, "I will make you proud."

I regretted the foolish boast as soon as I dismounted, landing in a nest of pebbles that made my moccasins slide straight down the moon-dark cliff.

As I tumbled down the rocky slope, I rousted a hooting owl from a nearby piñon and my buckskin warcap went flying. The javelina-skin quiver sailed off my back. My ceremonial arrows, painstakingly handcrafted from the hard wood of the mulberry tree, skewered the deep sand. Wildly I grabbed for some tree or boulder to block my fall, but there was nothing big enough to help me.

When I finally sprawled at the base of the cliff, blood oozed from my skinned knees and elbows, a tender lump throbbed on my temple, and a dozen fishhook cactus spines pierced my right palm. I could hear no sound in the darkness, nor see any brave's face, but I knew what the men were thinking.

No hope for this one. He is not fit to become an Apache man.

Silently I trudged back up the bluff, fighting the pain as I gathered my arrows. At least I could take pride in the fact that I had not cried out. But none of the others seemed to notice that. They were too worried about the owl.

"Did you hear it cry when the boy fell?"

"It is the ghost spirit warning us to turn back!"

CHAPTER ONE

"We cannot turn back!" Uncle Angry insisted. "We have hungry women and children waiting for us in the mountains!"

Scarred-by-a-Woman hotly disagreed. He was a wiry young man with four long, matching scars on his blade-hard face. Three years ago, he had been the one the warriors called Child-of-the-Water, the ritual name I had been given now. Nobody doubted his courage, but he was a cruel man, and a reckless one. He was also the younger brother of my cousin's husband, Cougar-Feet, which made us distant kin.

"We have a job to do," he growled to the others. "We cannot risk bad luck brought on by clumsy children."

I flushed red with shame and fury, but I knew it would be disastrous to challenge a seasoned brave. At fourteen winters, I was very young to be allowed the chance to prove myself as a warrior. I could not afford a great mistake.

"We have no men in our band to spare," Uncle Angry reminded Scarred-by-a-Woman. "Every boy must have his chance. Have you forgotten so quickly your time as Child-of-the-Water?"

Scarred-by-a-Woman all but sizzled. "Keep him well back from the Mexicans' lodge!" he ordered, as though it were his place to do so. "We need horses and cattle too much to lose them because of a boy with the feet of a white girl."

It was a terrible insult, and only my uncle's

fierce grip on my arm kept me from lashing out at Scarred-by-a-Woman. *Someday I will show him he's wrong*, I secretly vowed. *I will be the bravest warrior who ever lived!*

The braves argued for a few minutes more before deciding to go ahead with the raid we had planned. In eerie silence each one dismounted, handing me his buckskin lead. In the thick gray dawn I could almost see the warriors' faces, grim and determined, striped with white clay. Like me, they wore nothing but long breechcloths, flat warcaps and knee-high moccasins, but their bare arms rippled with hard-carved muscles I ached to own myself.

My uncle squeezed my shoulder lightly, then vanished with the others.

Imitating the warriors' soundless creeping, I led our unshod horses to the bottom of the cliff near the peeling red-bark trees. I knew that at first light the braves would spring up from the pastures of the Mexican ranch, mounting the grain-fed, rested horses they found there. They would herd the cattle around the bluff, away from their hidden novice warrior and winded ponies. Only when it was safe would my uncle return for me. Until then my job was to remain invisible.

The warriors only wanted to see me when there was work to do. On each of my raids I'd followed endless orders. *Gather the firewood, Child-of-the-Water. Carry the prickly-pear cakes. Use the sacred stick when you scratch yourself so your skin will not turn soft. Drink from the cut-reed tube so ugly hair will not darken your face. Never look back toward the village.*

It was difficult not to look behind me when trouble's hot breath always burned our ankles. Ever since our tiny band had ripped loose from the reservation in the spring, bluecoats had been stalking us with Chiricahua traitor-scouts throughout the land they called Mexico and Arizona. We did not care what names they gave it. We knew that *Yusn,* Giver-of-Life, had created it just for us. We belonged to it the way the strong roots of a live oak belong to its mighty branches.

In our country, piñon pines clung to high, blue mountains rising up from the desert. Bears and pumas hunted there. Coyotes howled. The white-eyes called it a hot, dry land of towering rocks and cactus, but we knew where to look for hidden water. We knew where to look for food. We knew how to hide ourselves and bury everything we might need later. The bluecoats could never track us without help from our own.

Pushing the traitors from my mind, I listened to the darkness, gently stroking each restless pony. Behind me some night creature darted through the dry-as-death underbrush, causing one horse to toss his head. Quickly I crept toward the uneasy beast and wrapped both hands around his silken muzzle, mutely soothing his fears and commanding him to silence.

Far to the east, I heard a puma scream, and I

stifled a chill as I calmed the jittery horses. My elbows and knees were growing stiff with blood and bruises. I wished—

Suddenly I heard it, the sound every warrior welcomes and dreads. A gunshot, then another, coming from the direction of the Mexican ranch! A moment later I heard the thunder of cattle and at least a dozen horses.

My heart began to thump as I heard the hooved beasts skip through a pass far to the south and head straight up the distant cliff. I knew that the warriors were moving fast, and I wondered anxiously what I would do if Uncle Angry were too hard pressed to come back to the peeling red-bark trees for me. I didn't dare leave on my own because there was always a chance that some of the men hadn't stolen good mounts and would need the weary ones I held in order to escape.

The sorrel at the end of the line raised his head and nickered. The black in the middle neighed loudly, a challenge in the night. I tried to quiet the black, but then the sorrel was calling too, and a long-legged roan started pawing the rocky earth.

The captured horses and steers were almost out of earshot now, but the sound of gunfire was moving closer. My fingers trembled. I knew something had gone wrong. It was unlikely that the Mexicans could catch up with the warriors, but this was their land and they surely knew every tree and crevice. They might swing around this way to cut off the raiding party! It was also possible that they were close on the heels of a fleeing brave, but it was not likely. Bringing the enemies' guns to my hiding place would put me in danger, and ordinarily our warriors' first priority was protecting Child-of-the-Water, whoever he might be.

But these were not ordinary times.

I did not know what to do. I could not risk failing to carry out my uncle's orders or bringing bad luck to our band, but neither did I want to die so young that I remained a child forever when I reached The Happy Place. The only fighting weapon I had with me was my knife, and it would not help me much against enemies with guns.

When thunderous bullets peppered the canyon just below me, wild darts of fear shot through my throat, my heart, my airless lungs. Desperate for action, I wrapped the rawhide leads around my elbow and drew my knife from its sheath. How close were the Mexicans? Were they searching for me or firing at my uncle? I couldn't hide with a half dozen horses. But how could I just stand there, waiting?

When a rifle-toting shadow burst from between two trees and threw itself at the ponies, the roan panicked and lurched against me, knocking my knife from my hand. It landed harmlessly on the enemy's left moccasin—which curled up over the toe, Apache style—then slid off.

Too late, I glanced up at the beaded warcap and realized I'd nearly stabbed one of our own! It was Scarred-by-a-Woman. Every breath he took was a desperate gasp. Blood rushed from his right leg as he hobbled toward the horses. I could not see his face, but I knew that his eyes were black with disdain.

Quickly I unwrapped the leads from my elbow and tried to steady the nearest horse for him. Without a word, he used his long rifle as a stick to brace his injured leg while he struggled to climb up on the sorrel. Then he jerked the line loose from me violently, wrenching the other rawhide leads from my hand. I swallowed a yelp as I sucked my rope-burned fingers and tried to catch the other leads before the ponies escaped, but I was too late and they scattered before me.

Wildly I ran after them, stumbling in the half-darkness, before the sound of gunfire exploded behind my ears. At once I dropped and flattened myself against the ground. Scarred-by-a-Woman raced off on the sorrel. I did not move as a half dozen horses roared past me, their riders hollering words in Spanish, which I did not understand.

Bruised and bloodied, I cowered in the dirt, terrified and humiliated that I had failed utterly to prove I was a man. I was alone in the land of the enemy—horseless, trembling—with nothing but a bow and four blunt bird-arrows in the quiver on my back. I begged Yusn for help, and he reminded me that it was the sacred obligation of every Apache warrior to rescue a fallen comrade who calls his name—even if the result was certain death.

"Scarred-by-a-Woman, help me!" I screamed, too desperate to be proud.

CHAPTER 2

IN THE TERRIBLE RUMBLE of hoofbeats and gunshots, maybe Scarred-by-a-Woman did not hear my plea. But it made no difference. He should have rescued me. He was an Apache warrior, and a warrior lived by his people's laws.

Every Apache child knew that when we were wronged, we made war to punish the guilty, and we killed all those who deserved to die. Geronimo, our strongest medicine man, had led so many successful expeditions to avenge our dead that all the white-eyes knew his name and feared him. But for him, and for the rest of us, raiding was quite different from warfare. We raided the way the white men farmed—to bring home food for our families.

In the old days, the only reason we let the white settlers stay near our land was so they could grow horses and cattle for us to harvest. They did not follow us when we took the animals if we killed no humans, so we were careful to raid that way. Swift and silent, we were gone before they knew there was trouble.

But Scarred-by-a-Woman often put his pride before his people, as he had done on his first full-warrior raid. It was the night he earned his name.

Discovering a young girl in a barn sleeping beside her sick colt, Scarred-by-a-Woman chose to kill her instead of slipping away unnoticed. She clawed his face with all her might as he stabbed her, and her blood mingled with his as she died.

As I listened to the still-thundering gunshots, I wondered how much I would bleed if the Mexicans came back to kill me. I wondered if my death would be avenged. I wondered if my adopted mother would cut her hair in mourning.

How she had begged me not to risk my life and leave her! I remembered so clearly the night last spring when my uncle—her only surviving brother—had slipped into our wickiup on the Fort Apache Reservation to tell us Geronimo's plan. A small group of us, mainly younger men and women and their children, would disappear in the night before the bluecoats suspected trouble.

The reservation was on White Mountain Apache land, far to the north of our own Chiricahua Mountains. Since we had been crushed by the white-eyes, we had lived on the reservation shoved together with all kinds of Apache bands. They were, more or less, our distant kin, but we were not really welcomed by them. Nor were we happy living wherever the bluecoats commanded.

Of all the Apaches, the Chiricahuas had

fought the longest and the hardest to stay free. But in the end, there were just too many greedy white-eyes. They had overrun us and seized our land. Now their leaders told us where to live and ordered us to farm.

But we were hunters. Raiders. Mountain people. Besides, we could not plant barren land with no tools or seed, and every time we tried to do what the white-eyes told us, they would move us somewhere else again.

The cruel years on the reservation had left us tattooed with numbers like the bluecoats' horses and begging for rotten meat. Our girls were not protected from the soldiers, and our boys were denied the right to learn what they must to become true men. Chief Naiche and Geronimo had tried to adjust, to obey, to keep promises that the white-eyes always broke, but it was not the Apache way to grovel for the enemy or live under his boots.

Finally our proud men could endure the starving and humiliation no longer. It did not matter, said my uncle, that the white-eyes believed our time was over, that there were no more free bands of Apaches or any other unchained tribal people. He had told my widowed mother that he would rather live as a free man for one mighty hour than to live a hundred years as a white-eyes slave.

She had refused to come with him.

I had refused to stay.

It was not because I did not love her. I had been a loyal son since she had found me, abandoned at birth, and named me Little-Left-Behind. When I was old enough to prove my honesty and obedience, Uncle Angry changed my name to Solito, All-By-Himself. He said it made me sound like a brave boy instead of lonely one. And he taught me that a brave man cannot always choose safety over freedom.

My uncle's son, Orejon, was my best friend, and we both knew that if we stayed on the reservation, we could never become true Apache warriors. Uncle Angry had taught us everything Chiricahua boys must know: the right words and rituals for hunting, how to make weapons, how to outwit the enemy and survive. Every day he made us get up early to run several miles and bathe in the river before dawn so we would always be clean and strong. When we were little, he taught us to ride horses and shoot tiny arrows at birds and bushy-tailed wood rats, and when we were older, he taught us how to "drum in" rabbits and bring down larger game.

Orejon and I had always planned to go on our first warpath together. But he was two years younger than I and his father said he was not yet ready to become a man.

As I crawled back to the shelter of the peeling red-bark trees, I realized that neither was I.

I do not know how long I shivered in the dirt before full dawn swept across the mountains. I prayed to Yusn to send my uncle back for me. I prayed for Angry-He-Spears-Bluecoats' safety, and for the safety of the other warriors. I even prayed for Scarred-by-a-Woman, though he had broken Apache law by leading the enemy to a novice-warrior's hiding place and abandoning him. He had never been particularly kind to any of us, but he was distant kin and a member of my band. Nothing meant more than that to me.

I guess nothing meant more than that to him, either, because the sun was barely up when I spotted the sorrel just fifteen feet away. I was astonished that, even injured, Scarred-by-a-Woman had the skill to move so silently. And I was astonished that he'd shaken off the Mexicans in such a brief time to come back for me.

I could see his face, dark and hard with disgust. He pressed the sorrel to my side, then held out his arm, elbow bent, so I could grab hold and swing up behind him.

I wanted to thank him for saving me. I wanted to apologize for nearly stabbing him. But the words lay thick and heavy on my frightened tongue, and before I could speak, he snarled, "You will never be a warrior, Little-Left-Behind! You are not strong enough to be a man."

His words gnawed at me unbearably during our long ride back to the hidden gorge where we had agreed to meet the other warriors. We slept little and moved fast. Scarred-by-a-Woman never complained about his bloody wound, never showed a hint of weakness, never asked me how I felt or what I wanted. I said nothing. I desperately wanted him to forget I was even clinging to the horse behind him, his long warrior's hair flapping in my face. I was afraid he would reveal my shame to the other braves, or speak against me in the council when I finished my fourth expedition. Except for my fear that something had happened to my uncle, nothing scared me more than the chance that I would be forbidden to continue my manhood training.

I should have had another fear, the fear that all true warriors carried with them day and night. It was not until we joined Uncle Angry and the others and swept on without rest to our rocky stronghold, high in the Chiricahua Mountains, that I understood how selfish I had been to worry about myself.

We knew several hours out that something was wrong, because Uncle Angry spotted lines of dark-skinned bluecoats marching toward our summer home. I could not see them at first. I had not seen many things that he had shown me on the way—hidden mule deer and secret pools of water, once a fast-moving she-wolf. The bluecoats' eyes were no better than mine, because we slipped away before they saw us and circled back to enter the camp safely.

We found our long-skirted women and small children huddled in our wickiups. They were bravely silent, but worry darkened their gaunt faces. Without speaking, my aunt put her arms around me and hugged me tightly, then greeted Uncle Angry the same way. He embraced her with strength and more tenderness than I had ever seen in him. They exchanged a few words that I could not hear before he turned and joined the group of men gathered around Geronimo and Chief Naiche. I was not yet a warrior, so I was not invited to join the men. I had to get the news from my cousin, Orejon.

"My mother says we will have to give up," he greeted me, nervously tugging on one big ear. "The bluecoats have taken our women and children!"

At first I did not understand him. Our women and children were all around me! Suddenly I saw a vision of my own mother. I felt a dull pain in my chest. In a voice that was far too high to be a warrior's, I asked my cousin, "You mean they took some of our people from the reservation?"

"They took them all!" Bitterness tore the words from his mouth. "Every Chiricahua left at Fort Apache! We are the only Chiricahuas left in Arizona!"

"My mother?" I whispered.

"General Miles had her seized with the rest of them. The bluecoats crammed them into the iron horse and sent them where they can never escape! They say it is a prison-fort that lies next to water that goes on forever, as far from our land as the iron horse can run."

I could not speak. I felt the panic of a wounded deer when the wolves have surrounded him, already slashing to bring him down.

"They say we will never find our families on our own, but they will take us to them if we surrender. Then we will live together, penned up in a bluecoat fort!"

I crumpled to the ground. I was weak and hungry from our many hard-riding days and sleepless nights, and my hands were shaking. My heart felt too stunned to beat. We could not give up! We could never surrender!

"If we do as we are told, the white-eyes promise that in two years, we will be allowed to come back home. But I do not believe them."

As I listened to my cousin, I stared at the raw, upthrust boulders that sheltered what might be our last camp as a free band. Uncle Angry had taught me that Yusn had created the Chiricahua Mountains for the Apaches and for no one else. He had created White-Painted Woman, and Lightning had fathered Child-of-the-Water, her son. Then Yusn had created *us* as part of this world, this magnificent, perfect land. Could we even *be* Apaches somewhere else?

The warriors talked all night, and in the morning, Geronimo forced himself to tell the bluecoats that we would meet with their Great Warrior Chief, General Miles, to talk about surrender. He did this only because our warriors wanted to protect their families who had been taken to the Big Water place called Fort Marion, on the other side of the white-eyes' world. Geronimo would never have surrendered if he'd had no one to worry about but himself. He was the toughest Apache who ever lived, and it stabbed me deep inside to see him walk with his head bowed down.

As we rode in heart-dead silence through the sweet, sharp smell of kinnikinnick and pine, I felt the agony of each and every warrior. Already I missed my country! I vowed to return someday, no matter what the bluecoats did to me. I *would* make one last raid! I would never surrender my Apache heart to the white-eyes. Someday I would be a warrior!

Someday I would prove myself as an Apache man.

CHAPTER 3

IT TOOK TWO OR THREE WEEKS for us to ride down from our beloved mountains, surrender to General Miles at Skeleton Canyon, and follow the bluecoats to Fort Bowie. We could have done it in half that time if we'd been on the run, but we were in no hurry to leave our country and start our lives as captives. We traveled armed, still tense, still ready.

But when we reached the brick-and-wood fort, the soldiers seized our weapons. They took our bows and arrows, knives, and guns. They stole our mules and horses. They killed our dogs. They told us we could not take cooking pots or blankets or ceremonial herbs and pollens. The bluecoats said they would give us everything we needed, but they said it in a way that made us feel that we would not live to need it very long.

The women and children were forced into wagons to ride from the fort to the iron horse. I was embarrassed that the bluecoats thought I was a child, like Orejon, and not a novice warrior. My cousin and I were shoved in behind his mother, his sister Makes-a-Good-Home, and her little baby. Makes-a-Good-Home was a pretty girl about my age, but ever since her marriage to Cougar-Feet, she had been considered a woman whom I must treat very solemnly. We were still close, in a distant, respectful sort of way, but I missed the fun we had had together when we were little.

When the soldiers chained Uncle Angry's hands and feet, he held perfectly still, his head high and proud, but I could see the shame in his eyes. Cougar-Feet could not control his hatred for the white-eyes, and twice he lunged at the bluecoats in spite of the chains.

All the other warriors were chained as well, except for Scarred-by-a-Woman and two other young braves who were tough but not very tall. I think the bluecoats thought a boy must be a certain age to be a warrior. Scarred-by-a-Woman had lived only seventeen summers, but he had long since ceased to be a child.

"Do you want to run away?" Orejon asked, turning big, frightened eyes on me as I watched the belching smoke of the iron horse, thundering toward us for the very first time.

It was not an idle question, and I did not want to answer it without thinking. I knew that a few of the young single men had slipped away the night before we'd reached the fort and planned to keep living secretly in the mountains. I didn't think the bluecoats knew. It was Geronimo's band they'd been after, and Geronimo's band they'd forced to come in. It would be some time before they understood that all the Chiricahuas had not been removed from Arizona.

"I do not think my mother would want me to become an outlaw," I answered quietly. "She is helpless in that fort by the Big Water. I am sure she is waiting for me."

It was true, but there was more to the truth than that. A week ago I had believed I was ready to live the warrior's life with no one to guide me. Now I knew I was far from ready. Maybe Scarred-by-a-Woman was right. Maybe I didn't have the makings of a man.

Orejon kicked a small rock with the curled-up toe of his moccasin. "Do you really think she is still alive? Do you think they will let any of us survive?"

Before he could answer, the soldiers started shouting orders and pointing at us with their long, gleaming rifles. I wanted to stay near Uncle Angry, but the warriors, all chained, were hauled away from the rest of us and shoved into a train car of their own.

I fought a wild panic as the bluecoats pushed me onto the iron horse two minutes later. It coughed and cried and wheezed in a haze of smoke, and then, incredibly, in a whirl of stomach-tossing motion. I was astonished by the strange, rigid slabs we were told to sit on! And I was shocked by the smooth touch of the open spaces in the moving walls that looked clear as air but felt as hard as rock. I had never felt so caged, so trapped, so helpless.

Even though we were disarmed, the bluecoats never let their guns stray from our grim faces. Without my weapons, I did not feel like a warrior, or even look like a boy who would soon become one. The only proof I still had of my impending Chiricahua manhood was my long, black hair.

There was no good place to sleep on the train, and by the time night fell, it smelled horrible since none of us could get off it to relieve ourselves. Many of the old people and children were sick from the swaying motion as well, and there was no way to clean up their vomit. The bluecoats kept the doors and windows closed at all times, and the late summer heat was almost as bad as the stench.

Orejon and my aunt were dozing, off and on, but I had been awake all night. I wondered why Makes-a-Good-Home's baby would not stop crying. I had lived in my uncle's wickiup next to Makes-a-Good-Home and her husband for many months and had never heard Sweet-Smiling-Boy wail like this before. I knew that the soldiers had not let my cousin bring extra wild mustard grass or bark of heart-leafed willow to keep him clean inside the cradleboard, and he was surely hurting and itchy inside his own filth. Still, the way his eyes stayed closed and his tiny mouth scrunched up while he yelled, I was afraid that something more might be wrong with him.

CHAPTER THREE

Makes-a-Good-Home sat near Scarred-by-a-Woman, who was her husband's younger brother. It was Scarred-by-a-Woman's job to take care of his brother's family since Cougar-Feet had been taken away in chains.

I wondered what Scarred-by-a-Woman would do if one of the bluecoats attacked Makes-a-Good-Home. It was the fear of all the women. My own fear was of the train itself, and of the unknown place it was taking us. It seemed alive, like a mountain lion, but I knew this rolling prison was not like any desert wild beast. It rumbled and roared, but not even the enemies-against-power of a great medicine man like Geronimo could bring it to its knees. We all knew we could not escape. No wonder the bluecoats left us alone while it was moving.

I heard Scarred-by-a-Woman tell Makes-a-Good-Home that only the Chiricahuas, and some Warm Springs Apaches who had befriended us, had been sent away. All the other bands at the Fort Apache reservation—Cibecues, Tontos, and White Mountain Apaches—had been allowed to stay. Geronimo helped lead the Chiricahua, and that was why the bluecoats wanted to punish all of us for the things Geronimo had done. I wondered if *they* would ever be punished for the things they had done to *him*.

I also wondered, for one traitorous moment, what would happen if I told the bluecoats that I was, by blood, not a true Chiricahua but a member of the White Mountain Apache tribe. I had no proof, but I had always believed it. My mother had found me, a newborn cast aside on the bloody ground, high in the White Mountains at a time when the bluecoats were at war with many Apaches. She'd never told me more than that, and I didn't know whether it was because she was not sure why I'd been abandoned or because she didn't like to think about the time when I was not her son but someone else's. Nor did she like to think about the fact that if she had not found me, I would have died.

But I had not died. I had become a Chiricahua. And whatever fate lay in store for my adopted people, I knew that I must bear it with them.

Suddenly Makes-a-Good-Home's hushed voice alerted me to trouble.

"No, do not leave us, Scarred-by-a-Woman!" I heard her whisper fiercely.

I knew something terrible was happening because she used Scarred-by-a-Woman's real name, instead of calling him "my husband's brother," which was the usual custom. But he ignored her plea.

"You can't jump out off the iron horse!" my cousin persisted. "You will be killed!"

"I cannot live this way. I am dead already," he snapped back hotly.

This was not the respectful way a warrior should speak to his brother's wife, but Scarred-by-a-Woman yelled at her anyway.

"You give this message to my brother."

"He would beg you not to go, as I do!" she pleaded. "Even if the fall does not kill you, where will you go? How will you live?"

"I am a Chiricahua warrior! I will live as my grandfathers did," Scarred-by-a-Woman arrogantly replied.

I was jealous of the strength I heard in his voice. I knew he really could survive on his own, just as I knew that I could not.

"But we have already left our country!" Makes-a-Good-Home pleaded. "You don't know where we are. You don't know how to get back home."

"I know I cannot remain a white-eyes slave for another hour!" His tone was brutal. "The bluecoats have put our warriors in chains and treated our women like animals! On the warpath, I have seen them kill our children! They would suck the very souls from our bodies if they could!"

I knew what he said was true, and so did Orejon's sister. But that did not change the fact that any man who jumped from the iron horse at full speed would probably be killed, and I didn't want anyone else in our band to die, not even Scarred-by-a-Woman, who might yet expose me as a coward. Still, I was thrilled by the notion that one last Apache brave had the courage to do something impossible, so daring that the bluecoats never expected it. I wished I had the courage to go with Scarred-by-a-Woman, but I knew that he was a war-honored veteran who would refuse to take me with him. I also knew that I did not have the courage to jump from a roaring monster.

Their conversation ended when Sweet-Smiling-Boy shrieked again, and Makes-a-Good-Home tried to soothe her desperate baby. As the iron horse clanged along, I stared outside but Moon did not help me probe the darkness. Daylight, a few hours ago, had revealed some sort of open prairie, utterly flat, even flatter than the part of our land that the white-eyes had named New Mexico. Only once on this long journey had I seen any buffalo, a tiny herd of maybe twenty animals. I had seen nothing else that might serve as game.

I marvelled at that. How did the white-eyes live all crowded together in the towns we had passed without any wild things to hunt? How could they live so far from running water? How could they conquer us when they had no souls and we were protected by the power of Yusn?

And then I forgot my questions, because Scarred-by-a-Woman used his mighty fist to smash through the clear space the bluecoats called a window. With the speed of a puma he crawled through the jagged hole and leaped out into the night.

CHAPTER 4

TWO DAYS LATER we stopped at a white-eyes village that had many wooden buildings and some that were made of the Mexican mud-brick we often saw in our own land. Many horses and wagons filled the streets, and hundreds of white-eyes ran along the rails of the train. At first I did not understand what they were doing. No one would choose to get near this putrid iron horse! But as we were prodded off by soldiers' rifles, I realized that these people had not come to see the train. They had come to stare at us.

They pointed. They jeered. They laughed out loud when my aunt stumbled and almost fell. Then they waved their short guns and rifles and screamed things that made me certain they wanted to kill us on the spot. The bluecoats moved closer together, but I was not sure whether they wanted to protect the white-eyes crowds from us or protect us from them.

I wondered who would protect us from the bluecoats. The morning after Scarred-by-a-Woman had jumped off, they had used an interpreter to question us cruelly about what had happened to our missing friend.

None of us had said a word. I had not even looked at Orejon or his aunt or his sister, and they had not looked at me. The bluecoats threatened to kill us if we did not talk—one drew his finger across my throat—but I'd held my ground. For once, I thought, Scarred-by-a-Woman would be proud of me.

Here in San Antonio, the bluecoats did not mention him. They paraded us into an old fort made of more Mexican-mud bricks. Like all bluecoat places, this one had a big red, white, and blue blanket hanging from a pole.

I was certain that they had taken us off the train to torture and then kill us in some special white-eyes way, and my heart thumped up in my throat as I considered the possibilities. It always took a long time for our warriors and old women to kill white-eyes who had been collected to pay for our murdered loved ones. We had no reason to expect bluecoat mercy now.

Makes-a-Good-Home pulled her fretting baby closer. She made no sound, but I saw tears in her black eyes. My aunt put an arm around her shoulder. Across the big square, I could see my uncle moving slowly with the other warriors, his head bowed down.

Orejon and I said nothing as the soldiers herded us toward a line of bluecoat teepees. It was hideously hot, and my headband was so full of sweat that drops were sliding down my forehead. I wiped them off quickly so my cousin would not think they were tears.

At last a bluecoat chief came to speak to us. A Mexican man who spoke Apache told us what he said.

"You will stay here tonight. Each family will have a tent. We will take the chains off the warriors, but if any one of you—man, woman, or child—tries to harm one of our soldiers or run away, we will kill you all."

The minute they unchained Uncle Angry, he rushed to stand in front of us, using his body as a shield to protect his family from the bluecoats. There was not enough room for his wife and children to cower behind him until I realized I should not be hiding but standing by his side. Quickly I took my place as a warrior, hoping that no one had noticed my delay.

Our chief, Naiche, spoke to us and told us to arrange ourselves in the bluecoat tents as we always did in each camp—family groups in neighboring wickiups, most honored warriors near his fire. Of course there were not enough tents for each family to have its own, so we had to share and make special arrangements to make sure that no man violated our sacred mother-in-law avoidance traditions, which forbid a man to enter any home when his wife's mother is there. It was very crowded in my aunt's tent, but since Uncle Angry was back with us, we did not complain.

Of course, there was still no way for us to bathe, and no way to escape from the soldiers' threats and the local white-eyes' craziness.

Outside the fort's front gate, cowboys and townsfolk shot off guns and tried to market fake bows and arrows and pretend-Apache knives to easterners. Some tried to get close enough to take pictures of us, selling them to anyone who would buy. They called *us* wild Indians, but I had never seen wilder people in my life.

Days passed, and then weeks, while we sweated and choked in the filthy little tents. We could not bathe or move the camp when the time came that it began to smell bad. The white-eyes gave us food, but it was not our kind. There was some beef, which we could eat, but also pork and turkey meat, which Yusn had forbidden us to touch. The hard bluecoat bread did not please our tongues or fill our bellies. It just kept us alive.

Worst of all was the waiting, the fear, never knowing if we would be alive or dead by the end of each day. We had no news of the white-eyes' plans for us. General Miles had promised that we would join our stolen families if we surrendered, but by now we knew we had been betrayed.

As my heart ached for hope, my body yearned for exercise. We could not run or ride or hunt or dance or play the camp games we all enjoyed so much, but at least Orejon and I could wrestle every day. At night my aunt would tell us tribal stories to remind us who we were.

It was too early to tell winter Coyote Tales, so she reminded us of courageous events in the lives of our people. My favorite was the story of a Chiricahua bride who escaped from the enemy after two years of slavery and walked hundreds of miles to return to her band, using the secret Apache supply caches hidden on the way.

Geronimo and the other warriors grew angrier each day that passed in this dismal place. One night the men gathered in Naiche's tent to talk about our situation. My uncle said I could come along as long as I sat respectfully in silence.

"Even though you have not yet proved yourself as a warrior," he explained, "you are almost a man. My son is too young and my daughter's husband may be taken away with me, so if more trouble comes upon our family, you must be prepared."

His words made me feel a great deal older than Orejon, and a little bit better about my last pathetic raid. Either Scarred-by-a-Woman had not told anyone what had happened before he jumped, or my uncle was willing to give me another chance anyway.

There was not enough room in the tiny tent for all of us, but we crowded in so the white-eyes could not see our council. We had no pipe, no pollen, and no fire inside—the bluecoats said it was so hot we didn't need one—and it was not possible to follow our usual ceremony. Still, we sat cross-legged in a circle. Geronimo sat at

Naiche's right, as his second, while the seasoned warriors pressed close on each side. Since my uncle was one of these, I could not sit by him. My back poked halfway out the tent flap, but I could hear and see everything inside.

"The interpreter tells me," Naiche said, "that we have stopped here in Texas because the bluecoats can not agree on what to do with us. Some of them want to send us back to Arizona, where the white-eyes could hang us for murder according to their laws. Some of them want to keep General Miles' promise to send us to our families at Fort Marion in the place called Florida." His voice dropped as he added, "And some of them want to kill us right now."

We all took time to consider his words.

"We agreed to surrender only so we could join our families," one of the men finally answered. "If that will not happen, we should escape."

"But how will we ever find our families?" another warrior questioned. "We have no idea what the white-eyes are doing to them. We must find a way to help them if we can."

"We cannot help them if we are dead!" Cougar-Feet protested. "If they plan to kill us, we must escape before they attack us here or stuff us back on the train."

"Scarred-by-a-Woman escaped from the train," Uncle Angry pointed out.

I knew he was upset with Scarred-by-a-

Woman for leaving our family unprotected on the iron horse, but he could not say this outside our family's tent.

"Only because the stupid white-eyes thought he was a boy and left him unchained."

"Do you think he will try to help us?" another warrior asked.

We all had to think about that for a while. I wanted to say that I had heard Scarred-by-a-Woman's last words and I knew he was only worried about himself, but it was not my place to speak.

Finally Cougar-Feet admitted, "When my brother abandoned my wife and baby, he made it clear he would not would follow the iron horse." His face grew dark with shame.

After a respectful silence, Geronimo said, "He is a Chiricahua warrior. He will survive. His moccasins know the way back to Yusn's land."

When we left the others, Uncle Angry took me to a far corner of the fort where no one else could hear. Then he said sternly, "There is a reason the bluecoats did not chain you, nephew. They do not understand that you are all but a warrior now. You are small in body, but Yusn knows that you are large in heart. If the white-eyes kill the men—*when* they kill the men—Yusn may protect you."

"Uncle, you must not speak of—"

"It must be said. If they kill me, and if they kill my daughter's husband, there will be no other man to protect my family. This job should have gone to Scarred-by-a-Woman, but he deserted his brother's wife and child. Now this duty falls to you."

I choked back a deep breath. This was the obligation of a man, not a child. I was proud. I was frightened. I was determined. I was overwhelmed.

Uncle Angry studied me for a long moment, then said gravely, "Solito, when I am taken, I leave my loved ones in your hands."

CHAPTER 5

THE NEXT DAY THE BLUECOATS routed us from our tents and prodded us with their rifles back to the iron horse. The warriors were chained again and forced into a train car apart from their families. This time I did not mind being placed with the women and children, as Uncle Angry had given me a warrior's job to do. We were all silent, as we had been taught, but we were certain that our men were going to be murdered. I prayed with all my soul for Yusn to keep my uncle from harm.

The white-eyes who lived in the town surrounded us again, screaming, laughing, calling us names that we did not need to speak their ugly language to understand. It was the same way each place we stopped for the next three days. Sometimes we crossed open fields. Sometimes we saw tall metal poles criss-crossed together so the white-eyes could steal something precious from Earth. Sometimes we saw white-eyes towns. As we traveled toward the rising sun, the land grew more and more watery until I was not sure whether the train was running on ground or swimming through a swamp. Once the iron horse stumbled and fell off its track. My aunt and Makes-a-Good-Home tried to comfort the little children while Orejon and I searched for a way to escape. We could find no way out, though, and after a lot of noise and fuss, the train went on its way.

Late one night, while we were all sleeping, the iron horse chugged to a ragged, lurching stop. Bleary-eyed, we waited for the soldiers to prod us off the iron horse, but no one came inside our train car, stifling hot and putrid even now in the middle of the night. No one opened the doors, but I could hear a strange sound, like liquid wind, battering the sand outside.

I glanced out the dirty window, but again, Moon did not help me to see. Shortly after dawn, I looked outside once more and realized that many white-eyes were gathering to stare at us again. This time there was something for us to stare at, too. The strange, windy sound I had heard in the night was coming from the Big Water that stretched out almost as far as I could see.

Had we finally reached Fort Marion in the land the white-eyes called Florida? Would I see my mother soon? Was it possible we had reached the end of this terrible journey?

I thought I could see a dot of land out in the folding lines of white-green water, but I could not be sure. Many white-eyes boats blocked my view. Closer to the shore I could see a curious kind of giant fish-creature, maybe five or six, leaping up and down as though they were doing some sort of a watery war dance. They looked happy, but their happiness couldn't change my deathly fear. I had always been taught that our dead turned into underwater animals. It was the reason we could not eat fish. Were these some of our people who had been brought here before? If the bluecoats had killed my mother, could she be swimming out there?

Suddenly Orejon cried out, "Look! The warriors!" and we both pressed against the window on the Big Water side of the train.

Two lines of bluecoats stood armed beside the train car that had been pulled off the track. Now our men stumbled out, one at a time. They were still chained. I saw Geronimo, Chief Naiche, Cougar-Feet, and finally Uncle Angry. He was wedged between two fierce-faced soldiers who pressed so close to him that it was hard for him to shuffle along.

The gawking white-eyes crowded around our warriors as the bluecoats marched beside them, and the white-eyes out in the water rocked their bobbing boats as they hollered things at us.

Orejon and I looked silently at each other, certain that this would be the end of our long journey, probably the end of our lives. Tensely we waited to join our men, but suddenly the steam and chugging noise started up again, and we realized that the iron horse was taking us away from them.

I could not believe it. Not only was I to lose my mother, but Uncle Angry too!

My aunt screamed his name. So did Orejon. Makes-a-Good-Home called frantically for her husband, her anguish so sharp it pierced me. Sweet-Smiling-Boy sobbed in the confusion. Everyone in our train car was banging on the windows, yelling for our braves, but the bluecoats would not let us go with them.

I pushed my way to a window and hollered for my uncle, even though I knew he could not hear me. Still, he could hear the sound of the iron horse, and as he turned around to see it go, I saw his resigned face, searching the grimy windows.

I saw him nod to my aunt, just once, as though to say goodbye. He lifted his chin to show his children he was not afraid. And then, for just a moment, he stared at me.

It was not "goodbye" I saw then in those sad eyes, or even "I'm proud of you, nephew." It was, *"Solito, only you can take care of my wife and children now."*

That was a message that one man gives to another, and it should have made me proud. But I felt overwhelmed by my assignment—if Uncle Angry could not defeat the bluecoats, how could I?—and I could not push away my grief. I was certain the bluecoats were going to kill him.

And maybe me, too.

Eventually, my fatigue and the rocking motion of the train lulled me into an uneasy sleep with my face pressed against the window. As the sun crawled up to the top of the sky, I began to dream.

I was not inside the train but outside on a fine, black horse with a blaze on his forehead and a full, flying mane. I was not wearing filthy rags but a new buckskin shirt—richly fringed and beaded—that my mother had made especially for me. I wore painted wrist guards and bright earrings of silver and the blue that comes from Earth. My moccasins were soft, new ones that wrapped my feet and legs clear up to my knees. I galloped beside the iron horse, matching it mile for mile, until suddenly one of the bluecoat guards looked out the window and saw me.

He smashed a window with his rifle butt, but his bullets could not find me. I raised one hand to stop them, and with the other, pulled out my knife from the sheath on my green and yellow woven sash-belt. At once my hair came loose from the back of my breechcloth, where it was neatly tucked, and blew magnificently in the wind. It was dark and thick and smooth and told the world I was a warrior of great strength and power.

As my hand closed upon the knife, it changed to wood and grew into a magnificent mulberry-wood bow. My lucky cougarskin quiver held four bird arrows, too small and blunt for a novice to kill a bluecoat. But as I drew one out it brushed the feathered medicine cord flying across my chest and instantly became an Enemies-Against-Power arrow that would kill any enemy it struck. I shot it at the soldier and he fell, even though he was too far away for the arrow to pierce. More soldiers rushed to the broken window, and I shot each one with the same magic arrow, and it kept flying back to me.

When all the soldiers were dead, my people started pouring out of the broken window. I recognized their faces: Orejon, Makes-a-Good-Home, Sweet-Smiling-Boy, my mother, my aunt, my aunt's mother, a scrawny old medicine man named One-Who-Remembers, and all the others we had left on the reservation! They told me they had been waiting for me in the terrible bluecoat fort on the edge of the Big Water.

"We knew you would save us!" they called out to the beat of a victory dance drum. "You are the last Chiricahua warrior!"

I felt proud and strong. This was not a raid but a valiant warpath rescue which would serve as my fourth expedition and confirm my place as a true warrior.

But as I got all the women and children together, I heard another voice inside. It was my Uncle Angry, and I could see him through the train walls, chained to the wheels that clanked round and round so fiercely.

"Solito, my nephew, do your duty!" he cried. "Save my wife and children!"

When he used my name, I could not say no, even though suddenly there were hundreds—no, thousands!—of bluecoats murderously surrounding the train. Bravely I flew off my horse and pressed toward the shattered window, but it had healed now and locked itself shut. Although I pounded and banged upon it, it would not budge.

My bow suddenly shrank back to the size of a knife and my magic arrow disappeared. My clothes were shabby and my hair was chopped off in front as a symbol of mourning. I could not help my uncle. As the train bolted forward, I fell on the tracks and the mighty wheels ground me to dust along with him.

Abruptly I woke up as the iron horse screamed and skidded on the rails, and I realized that we had stopped again.

CHAPTER 6

THIS TOWN, AT FIRST, seemed no different from the others we had passed through. While all the white-eyes made fake Indian noises and stared as they had done in every other town, the bluecoats once more used their rifles to nudge us through the streets like cowboys herding longhorn cattle.

"The white-eyes buildings here look like some of the ones the Mexicans make back home," Orejon glumly observed as he trudged through the streets in his worn-out moccasins.

He was right. They were low buildings, made of some kind of clay or stone with sharp corners. Only a few were made like fort-houses, using wood or heavy stone.

I nodded, trying to ignore the shouts of the white-eyes who now followed us. Our interpreter told us some of the things they said.

"Show us a war dance!"

"Ain't you savages never heard of a bath?"

"Lookee that squaw! I think she likes me!"

I would have killed them all if I could, but there was nothing I could do but show the others how to act—too proud to let the white-eyes' words touch our hearts. What did we care what they thought of us, anyway? They were not Apaches; they had no souls. They did not know the ways of Yusn.

The air smelled better than it did on the iron horse, but it had a salty tang to it, a smell I had never known back home. The sky felt almost wet, even though it was very hot and there was no rain. I realized that it would be hard to run away from this place. To run like the wind, an Apache must breathe.

How could I breathe in this solid stone fort before me? It was huge and ugly. It smelled of rotting meat and green-slick mold. Bluecoat tents perched on top of a partial rock roof, bordered by a fierce-looking thick wall that surrounded the prison. The fort lay so low on the land that it almost seemed to swallow the endless water, and noisy white birds circled around it, alarming us with their grating cry. Never had I longed so fiercely for the desert, for the dry, clean heat of my home.

Orejon's lips were quivering, so I took a step closer to him. After we crossed a large, flat bridge, we slipped on wet stone into a manmade cave.

"They cannot mean to leave us here!" Orejon whispered, fighting wetness in his eyes. "We cannot live in this steaming cage."

I did not know what to tell him. I had promised Uncle Angry I would do my best to protect his family, but at the moment there seemed to be nothing I could do. My hands trembled, and my soul shook with foreboding. If I ran now, the bluecoats would surely shoot me. Would that not be a better death for an almost-warrior, a quicker trip to The Happy Place?

But even if had the courage to face their guns, I did not have the courage to face Uncle Angry's ghost if I failed to keep my promise. So I dragged myself forward into the dungeon, even though I was certain that it was the place where I would die.

It was dark below the stone walls. Behind me, I heard the voices of the local white-eyes yelling their disappointment that they could no longer see us, could no longer point and jeer. I tried to close my ears to them. I prayed to Yusn to help me in any way he could.

And Yusn answered. In my own tongue. I was so startled to hear an Apache voice calling from a distance that it took me a moment to realize that it was a real person, one of my own people, and not one of us who had just been herded into this cave.

"They are here at last!" someone shouted in Apache.

I knew the quavery old voice. It was our oldest medicine man, bone-thin One-Who-Remembers! He was still alive! And if he lived, surely some of the others might have survived!

Suddenly we were running, and not because the soldiers told us to. Our ragged group burst into the bright light of a grassy courtyard filled with Apache men wearing breechcloths and curled-toe moccasins . . . Apache babies in willow-branch cradleboards . . . Apache women in buckskin blouses and calico skirts!

All of a sudden I saw faces I'd known all my life, faces I would have known anywhere. These were my people! They were here, alive, and welcoming us! We might be in prison, but we were still a tribe!

It was not the Apache way to make a noisy display upon greeting family or friends, but this was not like any other time in our lives. This was a time to celebrate the return of loved ones almost from the dead.

I saw Makes-a-Good-Home rush to my aunt's mother, She-Lives-Longer, so old and wrinkled that there was surely not a smooth part of her face. She-Lives-Longer picked up Sweet-Smiling-Boy's cradleboard and tenderly held her great-grandson close. Because of the bluecoats, it was the first time she had ever seen him. She wept as she thanked Yusn for sending her this most precious gift.

My aunt and Orejon ran to hug She-Lives-Longer also, but I held back because I was looking for my mother, and I knew that if I asked where she was before She-Lives-Longer was ready to talk to me, the old one would scold me for my rudeness.

Everyone around me was glowing with joy and relief. Fathers found children, husbands found wives, brothers found sisters, and finally, after I searched every inch of the big plaza where we were allowed to mingle, I found the dear female face I so desperately sought.

"Mother!" The word ripped loose from my throat, my voice embarrassingly high and squeaky. As she reached for me, I watched tears gush unceasingly from my mother's loving, black eyes. Unashamed, I clung to her while she wept and wept. In spite of my almost-warrior pride, I felt wet streaks on my face as well.

"You are well? They have not hurt you?" my mother begged.

I shook my head and held her close. She looked older than when I had seen her last. Her face was far more wrinkled and there was no luster to her hair.

"I am not injured. I am angry, so angry that I have no words for what is in my heart. But I am not hurt and I am not dead."

She hugged me again, so tightly that her long fingers practically bruised my shoulder blades. She wore a very old buckskin dress with many rips and missing beads, but she wore no earrings or shells around her neck. She felt frail to me, too thin, and she coughed while she cried.

Finally she let me go and looked achingly into my eyes. "My brother, Angry-He-Spears-Bluecoats?" she whispered, the urgency of the situation forcing her to use his actual name. "He is no longer with you?"

I patted her arm, knowing there was little I could do to shield her from the truth. "He was alive and well this morning when the bluecoats took him off the train."

She hung her head and wept again, and this time, as I studied her broken form, I realized that it was not just grief that bowed her shoulders.

"Mother, you are not well!"

She shook her head and tried to straighten, but I could see it was hard for her to do.

"I cannot breathe here. I have no strength. I worked so hard to hold on until you came." Her eyes were blurry now. "I knew that one way or another, you would come back to me before I died."

CHAPTER 7

WE WERE ASHAMED of how we looked and smelled that night, but our people told us that they understood what had happened because the bluecoats had locked them inside the iron horse, too. Some of the babies and old people had died because of the scalding prairie heat, and others had passed away since the first of our people had arrived.

There was no river for us to bathe in, and we were not allowed to go out into the monstrous sea. There were two big metal pots; not for cooking, we were told, but for bathing, and we lined up for hours until we all could use them. The white-eyes had not given us clothes but our people at the fort had a little more than we did, so they shared what they could.

Even though we were all weary beyond human words, we were so happy to be together again that the old ones said we must have a celebration and a "thank-offering" dance. The women started cooking what little they had, and One-Who-Remembers brought out his medicine stick for the ceremony. I was surprised that the bluecoats at Fort Apache had let him bring it, but he told me that only the renegades who had been tracked down and forced to surrender had been forbidden to bring anything with them. The peaceful families torn from their new farms at Fort Apache had been able to bring basic things—food, sleeping skins, ceremonial paints, pots and pans. But they were ordered to leave their dogs and livestock behind, and had been given no time to gather many of our sacred herbs and pollens.

It was wonderful to hear the tribal drum again. After One-Who-Remembers told us how to best thank Yusn for bringing us back together, we danced in a big wheel, all facing toward the center. The older children got to do this, too, but I did not see many of the Chiricahua boys and girls my age that I had known at Fort Apache, and this troubled me. My aunt danced, and so did my married cousin, but my mother and She-Lives-Longer were not well enough to join us.

In between the dances, She-Lives-Longer listened gravely to my aunt's story of our surrender and then told us everything that had happened to our people at Fort Marion before we had arrived. The first Apache men and boys to come to the fort had been sent to an island just beyond us, were left there with almost nothing to eat and were told to fish. Fish! They would have died before they broke the eating taboos of Yusn, and they had nearly starved to death. Some of the others had lived down in the wet dungeon before the bluecoats crammed all the tents on the tops of the fort's rock roof. At least now each family had a tiny "home" and some fresh air and sunshine.

In a very quiet voice, my mother added that some of our people were angry with those of us who had escaped from the reservation with Geronimo because they blamed him for their own situation. They had not been happy at Fort Apache, but it had certainly been better than this! They longed to return to their own land, or at least close to it, and they believed that they would not have been ripped away from their country if Geronimo had not angered the bluecoats again.

She-Lives-Longer said she believed the white-eyes in Arizona would have found a way to get rid of us anyway, since they never ran out of ways to cheat us. She also told us something that truly frightened me.

One day, without warning, the bluecoats had come to steal our children. They said they wanted to teach the young ones how to be white-eyes, how to be happy, how to be strong. Our people had begged and begged not to be separated from their children, but the bluecoats had wrenched them away so fast that some had left without proper clothing. They had managed to hide a few and, by pretending that many men had more than one wife, trick the bluecoats into leaving some of the older girls. Now that more children had arrived, She-Lives-Longer cautioned, the same thing might happen again.

CHAPTER SEVEN

All that night, the men danced and the women talked and the children ran around the big grassy courtyard surrounded by the tall stone walls. I was very happy. Yet, inside, I grieved for Uncle Angry and the other men. Our celebration could never be complete when they were far away in chains!

At first I was so glad to see my people that I didn't notice how bad things were at Fort Marion. But soon enough I realized that there were hundreds of us crammed into a space big enough for one small band of twenty. The stone was always damp, and with autumn coming on, we were often cold. The mosquitoes feasted on us, day and night, and the soldiers reduced our issues of beef, bread, and hominy—and the useless pork which was taboo—shortly after I arrived.

It was obvious that many of our people were very ill. Most of them were not witched or suffering from ghost-sickness. It was the white-eyes disease that made them cough so much and struggle to breathe. Some spit up yellow phlegm from deep in their chests. Some could not hold down food, and others could not eat.

My mother was one of these. At night I listened to her as she slept, and every breath sounded like a horse that has been run to death. Geronimo was the greatest medicine man of our people, and I was certain he could have helped her, but we had to make do with One-Who-Remembers, who did his best though he seemed to have lost a lot of his power. Worst of all, he did not have the medicine plants Yusn gave us to heal the sick. Since he could not sprinkle my mother with cattail pollen, he could only spit in the fire and command the sickness to leave her body while the drum thudded and the bull-roarer buzzed. The dancers came up to her, waved their wands, and blew on her. Everyone prayed to Yusn. But without the pollen, the ceremony did not work, and she grew weaker every day.

The bluecoat fort doctor's medicine did not work either, but this did not seem to worry him. He was not unkind, but he could not see what my mother meant to me. He only saw another elderly Apache. He listened to her rattling chest and said she needed warm clothes, good food, and dry air. I asked the interpreter to tell him she could receive none of these things in this land they called Florida, but all were possible back home.

"She has done nothing!" I begged again and again. "Please send her back to her own country. She needs the dry air and the sight of her own land. She never rode with Geronimo. You can punish me as you like, but let her go!"

"There are no Chiricahuas left in Arizona," the interpreter reminded me. "Even if they granted her freedom, where would she go?"

I did not point out that Scarred-by-a-Woman would be there, if he had made it back alive, and that several of our other young braves had escaped from the soldiers before we were put on the train at Fort Bowie.

"There are still White Mountain Apaches at Fort Apache," I pointed out instead. "Their land has always bordered ours, and we managed to live with them on the reservation before the bluecoats sent all of us here. She could go back there."

I even explained about the time she had been living near some White Mountain Apaches and found me as a baby, but the story meant nothing to the bluecoat doctor. The Chiricahuas had been exiled from Arizona, and the white-eyes there did not want a single one of us to return. Even the Chiricahua traitor-scouts who had helped the bluecoats track us had been sent to prison as their reward, instead of the land and safety they'd been promised. We thought it was fit punishment for their betrayal, but it proved again that the white-eyes always lied.

My mother's health was not my only problem at the fort. As the days passed, I found myself wildly restless and bored. I was in the prime of my life, as fit and strong as any boy who ever lived, and this was the summer when I should have joined the men as a full-fledged warrior after proving myself in one last raid. Instead I was trapped in this horrible, stinking, wet cage—humiliated and defeated by the enemy. The sight of endless salt water to the east, ever flowing, ever free, only intensified my hatred.

So did the sight of the white-eyes, who still came to gawk at us every day. There were so many of them that the soldiers only let a few in to the fort at a time, but the rest stared at us from across the moat.

The ones that did come in spoke only English, which we did not understand. But our interpreter would tell us things. They wanted to see us dance, to shoot arrows, to look ferocious like trained bears poked with a stick. Of course, we could not do any of our sacred dances in the presence of white-eyes, but we ignored them while we played shinny, a wonderfully rough game in which we hit balls and each other with long sticks. Sometimes we also played hoop-and-pole, but this was harder to do in prison since it was taboo for women to be near the hoop-and-pole playing field, and that meant white-eyes women, too.

Some of the white-eyes who came to stare wanted to buy things we made. This made our captors happy, because these tourist-white-eyes also spent a lot of money while they visited nearby St. Augustine. We were allowed to make weapons to sell to them because the bluecoats no longer considered us a threat without our best warriors and the hiding places of our desert and mountain home. A few of our people who had been at the fort a long time were even allowed to go into the town under guard. There they could buy us things with white-eyes money—things we needed desperately, like blankets and food and clothes. When we lived in our own country, we always had plenty of these things, but we never had enough at Fort Marion.

Orejon and I helped One-Who-Remembers to make bows and arrows, partly because the tribe needed the money we made from selling them and partly because neither of us were very good at it yet. I had started making my own arrows shortly after I had killed my first deer and eaten its heart to make me strong. But Uncle Angry had taught me that the difference between a wobbly feathered arrow and one that was straight and strong could make the difference between life and death to an Apache.

I would need those straight arrows, plenty of them. Somehow I had to find a way to store food, collect blankets, hide weapons, and come up with a plan to lead my family on a daring escape.

I had made a promise to Uncle Angry—alive or dead—and I could not keep it here.

CHAPTER 8

ONE DAY, when we had been at the fort a few weeks, Orejon and I got to join the men when they went into St. Augustine to sell our handmade Apache goods and shell-trinkets. None of us liked the idea of peddling our work to white-eyes strangers, but we liked the idea of freezing and starving even less.

It was the first time I had gone across the moat since our arrival. There were about a dozen of us, as clean as two tubs shared by five hundred people could make us, but still wearing desperately old and tattered rags. We were not allowed to bring any weapons, but One-Who-Remembers assured us that the guards kept the white-eyes at a distance.

Except for my time on the train, I had never been in a white-eyes town before. It frightened me. The buildings were as tall as the fort walls—some even taller—so solid and hard that a person inside them surely could not breathe. On the main path, there was no ground beneath our feet, just broken white shells of some kind that my mother told me drifted in from the sea.

There were no cactus plants or desert

ocotillos. No high mountain firs or pines. I spotted a few trees that were very tall and had no leaves until way up at the top, where some long green strips flapped about like wings. Even though it was the Moon-of-Sizzling-Snow back home, here there were many flowers, bright red and purple and the color of the turquoise that Yusn left for us in his mountains. Their smell was very strong and they were all new to me. I saw no golden poppies, no chuparosas, no long-stemmed purple beardtongues.

There were fruits of all kinds and colors in boxes and on tables on the street where white-eyes people sat or stood and sold them to strangers. We did not understand how people could take money to share food with their own people! This was not our way. A rich Apache was one who raided well enough that he always had plenty to give away. Those warriors who did not share received no respect from our people and never led us in peace or war.

Orejon and I spotted some white-eyes boys our age playing bluecoat-ball in a grassy field. We had seen the soldiers play this game at Fort Apache, but we did not understand it. One boy would throw the ball at another one, who carried a thick stick. The second boy tried to hit the ball, and when he did, he started running in a square. Sometimes other boys caught the ball and sometimes they didn't. They almost never hit each other in the head with the ball, which showed us how poorly they'd been taught to bring down quail and opossums. Years before I had killed my first deer, I had used stones to bring this fresh meat home.

It was still daylight, but growing cloudy, when we started back to our people. As we neared Fort Marion, I realized that in spite of my prison life, I had enjoyed this day outside—a chance to walk in fresh air, if not to run.

And then, quite suddenly, I was jarred by the sounds of Apache terror beyond the ugly white-eyes walls.

The women were screaming. I could hear heavy-heeled footsteps, children running, men yelling in fierce Apache words that they rarely said out loud. At once the guards moved in closer, but we ignored them. We did not run away. We ran toward the fort. We had to see if we could help our people.

"What's wrong?" One-Who-Remembers hollered as soon as the gates were opened. "Where is my wife?"

A very old woman who had no one left rushed to him and said, "They are not hurting the women. They are stealing more of our children!"

I looked at Orejon and saw him shake with terror. I felt so helpless! I could do nothing for him or for any of the others. I ran to find my mother. She was rushing toward the dungeon, searching for me with frantic eyes.

I ran to her, but a giant bluecoat with a yellow beard caught my long warrior's hair from behind. I fought him, but he was too strong, and he had seized me by surprise. Still, I kept trying to wriggle loose, using my right foot to try to flip him over. I was furious that I could not wrestle him to the ground the way my uncle had taught me.

My mother ran to the interpreter, begged him for help, told him that I was all she had left and would die at Fort Marion without me. He told her that the yellow-bearded bluecoat said he had come for us because he wanted to give the Apache children a wonderful new life that they could never have with their own people.

My mother spit in the bluecoat's face.

"I will not go!" I screamed.

"It will be good for you," the interpreter relayed to me. "You will go to a special place where they will teach you how to live like a white-eyes."

"I do not want to live like a white-eyes!" I roared. "What can they teach me besides how to break apart families, how to cheat and lie?"

The wailing from the others filled the old fort walls. A friend of my aunt's slipped her long, full skirt over the head of her small daughter and hid her from the bluecoats' view. Another hid her son in a big rain barrel, but a white-eyes found him anyway. They seized Orejon, but they left Makes-a-Good-Home because she was married and holding Sweet-Smiling-Boy as proof of that. When the bluecoats were done, the only children left were tiny ones and those so sick that we already knew they would die.

My mother sobbed as the bluecoats dragged

me away from her. I heard my aunt scream. She-Lives-Longer hobbled out of our tent and pleaded for Orejon. Even the old men, normally so proud and silent, could not still their tears.

But the bluecoats ignored our pleas and took the children anyway. If they knew they were tearing our hearts from our chests, they gave no sign.

This time the train took us to a giant boat that pressed out into the mighty blue sea, rocking and rolling so much that I grew sick at once. I embarrassed myself by losing what little food had been in my stomach. The yellow-bearded bluecoat officer came over with a small white cloth to try to clean me up.

Now that I was not fighting him, he did not act unkind, but I could not forgive him for what he'd done. He spoke to me in English, without heat, but I did not know what he said to me and I did not want to. I thought of jumping off the boat, but I could not swim forever and I was not sure that I would reach The Happy Place if I drowned. All my life I had seen people die in the mountains and be sent to rest according to the laws of Yusn. Everything a dead person loved was burned, and even his best horse was killed to carry him to The Happy Place. No one could burn my things out here on the water, and the bluecoats at Fort Bowie had stolen our ponies.

Once we reached land, it took hours to cross through a huge city, much worse than

St. Augustine, riding part of the way in a fancy white-eyes carriage pulled by horses. It was almost dark again when we were beckoned onto another train. There were no extra guards now, and Yellow-Beard opened the windows so we could breathe.

The next time we stopped, hours later, he ordered us into wagons. Orejon sat close to me, and a smaller Apache boy wedged in on my left. Yellow-Beard tried to put the girls with us, but we refused. No decent Apache boy would press his body against a girl's—front, back, or side. Our girls had lost their families and all their dreams in this last capture. Their reputations were all they had left, and we were terrified that the bluecoats would take even this from them.

I could not see the land well in the darkness but it was free of the disgusting scorched-oil and too-many-people smell of the giant city we had passed through earlier. The air was lighter and easier to breathe than it had been in Florida. Frogs and crickets sang in the night. I heard a poorwill cry, which meant bad luck to Apaches, but at least I heard no ghost-owls. There were mosquitoes, but not as many as at Fort Marion, and they did not bite so hard.

Although night had long since fallen, Moon showed us the new fort as we pulled in. The buildings were made of brick and wood and looked like some of the Arizona bluecoat forts, only this one was much, much bigger. Except for the wide, grassy spaces, it could almost have been a small town. I could hear the horses nicker from the stables and a lone cow bawl. The one thing I did not hear was the sound of bluecoats, drilling or swearing or singing. I heard no human sound at all.

Then a painted wooden door opened as we crawled off the wagons, and I saw a small, older bluecoat who was not very tall but old enough to have white hair. I knew he would take charge of us because he carried himself like a chief. Yellow Beard urged us toward him, and we did as they asked. We were all too tired to fight.

An older Apache boy I had known on the reservation stood silently beside the old chief bluecoat. He had never been Child-of-the-Water, and back at Fort Apache, he had tried so hard to learn to farm and please the white-eyes that we had secretly called him White-Man's-Dog. I did not know how long he had been in this place, but he certainly no longer looked like an Apache. White-Man's-Dog wore bluecoat trousers and a bluecoat jacket, buttoned right up to his neck. He wore no headband, breechcloth, or knee-high moccasins, and his hair was so short he was practically bald. Imagine, a bald Apache! If we had not been so tired and frightened, we would have laughed at him.

When the bluecoat chief spoke to us, I did not know what he said, but it was clear that he wanted us to do whatever he told us without complaint. When he finished talking, he nodded to White-Man's-Dog, who spoke to us in our native tongue.

"This is the chief of Carlisle School. His name is Captain Pratt. He is the one who decides what will happen here. He will be good to you if you do what he says. He will punish you if you do not. You are to speak only English as soon as you can. You will learn how to dress like a white man, how to eat like one, how to read the white man's books and worship his own Giver-of-Life. The boys will learn how to farm and work at white man's jobs. The girls will learn how to take care of a white lady's house. These lessons will start tomorrow. We will take pictures of you now, and then you will be washed and given a place to sleep."

None of us moved. We asked no questions. We scarcely breathed. How I wished I had died a warrior's death in Arizona! I could imagine no worse fate than to be whitemanized like White-Man's-Dog, to become the white man's slave.

CHAPTER

9

TWO WHITE-EYES WOMEN led away the girls. Then White-Man's-Dog—who told us that the white-eyes called him "Steven" now—took us to a large, cold room where they had big kettles full of almost-boiling water. We knew they were for baths since we had shared similar tubs at Fort Marion. But we were not in the habit of revealing our nakedness to anyone, not even boys our own age, and there were dozens of us in this open room. The younger boys were silent, and I knew they were waiting to see what I would do.

The white-eyes man in charge had a dried up, homely face that reminded me of an overripe pumpkin. He gestured for me to take off my breechcloth, but I would not do it while he watched.

He said something to me in English, then repeated it in an angry tone. When my back stiffened and I refused to speak, he turned to Orejon instead.

Pumpkin-Face motioned for my cousin to come stand before him. I wondered if there was some sort of ceremony required before a white-eyes took a bath, and Pumpkin-Face was the one who must perform it. I felt uneasy, trapped, but bound by my vow to protect my family. I could see that Orejon was shaking.

And then I spied it—a sharp metal two-pronged tool that Pumpkin-Face was pointing at the top of Orejon's big ears. I felt a sudden stab of panic as I realized that he meant to take my cousin's scalp!

In that instant, Orejon screamed my name in a plea which certain death could not keep me from obeying. I threw myself at Pumpkin-Face and seized his bulky wrist, tossing the scalping tool to the ground.

He outweighed me, but I had been trained to kill by Uncle Angry. I threw myself at his chest with all my might and knocked him on his backside. He screamed as he went down. His head banged harshly on the wooden floor and the scalping tool skittered away.

Pumpkin-Face grabbed my arms as I seized his throat, but he was not strong enough to push me off. As I tightened my grip, the door slammed open and two big boys from different tribes bolted in and grabbed me, one by each arm. A second later the bluecoat chief called Captain Pratt rushed in behind them, just as they managed to pull me away.

He stood perfectly still, unarmed, and barked at me in English. I did not know what he said, but I knew he was very angry. What difference did it make? What punishment could compare to scalping?

White-Man's-Dog rushed up beside him.

Quickly he shouted at me, "Do not fight them! They do not mean to hurt you. This man only means to cut your hair."

I did not believe him. "He will have to kill me to cut my hair!" I yelled. "Have you ever seen a bald Apache warrior?"

White-Man's-Dog's lips tightened into a cold line. I knew I had insulted him, but I did not care. I was so angry and hurt and frightened that I wanted to explode. All I had ever wanted was to make my uncle proud, to ride strong and true as a man among my people! What had I ever done to make the white-eyes destroy my life? What would it take now for me to ever feel whole again?

I could have stabbed the chief and made my getaway, but I could not leave Orejon, who was still trembling behind me. The younger boys further back were deathly silent, unsure of what to do. I knew they would follow my lead.

Captain barked another order, and White-Man's-Dog relayed his words. "He says to act like a good white boy."

"I am not a white boy!" I shouted. Loud and long, my voice filled the room with our piercing warcry. "I am an Apache warrior!"

The bluecoat chief demanded a translation. When he got it, he took a step closer and said something hard and mean to me. White-Man's-Dog said, "He says he will make a good white boy out of you before you leave here, and tonight you will lose your wild Indian hair."

A true warrior, I knew, would have fought him to the death. But I wasn't one, and I feared that Scarred-by-a-Woman was right: I never would be. I had bolted into a rage because I thought Pumpkin-Face was going to kill Orejon. Now that I knew he wasn't, I felt foolish and ashamed.

"Show them how to act brave," White-Man's-Dog ordered. "I had this done to me. So have all the others in this place. It will only hurt your pride."

My stomach rolled. White-Man's-Dog had once been a true Apache boy, trained for a warrior's life just like me. What had happened to him here? Would I look like him and act this spineless after the white-eyes were done with me?

I looked behind me at the other boys. They leaned forward tensely in their shabby moccasins, ready to run. If we ran, where would we go? Could I take care of so many younger ones? And what about the girls?

Suddenly I realized that I must plan my escape with care, and I could only rescue Orejon. It would take all the skill I possessed to bring even one frightened boy back to his imprisoned mother . . . and somehow find a way to lead the rest of our family back home to safety.

"Endure, Solito," I could almost hear Uncle Angry calling to me. *"Wait. Plan. Protect your people."*

I straightened slowly, shaking off the hands

of the two boys at my sides. I ignored the heat that burned my heart and showed on my reddened cheeks. I walked back to Pumpkin-Face and forced myself to stand bravely before him. I met his eyes and would not look away. I let him see my hatred. I still vowed to kill him, in my own time, in my own way.

He picked up the scalping-tool from the corner where it had fallen. He shoved it above my left ear and scraped it backwards. For several long minutes, he cut and snipped without a word, while every Apache boy in the room watched my lifetime of almost-warrior's hair fall away.

I lived through the bath. I did not speak when they stuffed me into bluecoat clothes and stole my breechcloth and moccasins. Surely, I hoped, we would soon be locked into our new cage where I could mourn my latest loss with Orejon. But the bluecoat chief had something else in mind.

He took my arm and led me into a small room that had a white-eyes table and many pictures on the walls. A short black whip hung between two of them.

He did not sit down, and neither did I. With White-Man's-Dog still at his elbow, the captain spoke harshly to me. Of course I did not understand him. I had to wait for the translation by White-Man's-Dog.

"The captain says you are new here and

need some time to understand our ways. For that reason, he will not punish you for what you did tonight. He knows you are afraid. But he will not tolerate rudeness to any of the people who work here, and he will not allow you to practice your heathen Indian ways. He wants to help you learn to be happy here, but he cannot do this if you fight him. Next time you cause trouble, you will be whipped." Then, in a somewhat softer tone, White-Man's-Dog added, "He means what he says."

I did not look at either one of them. I said nothing while the captain motioned for me to follow him back to the others, who now stood in lines. They had been arranged by size, from the largest to the smallest ones, so Orejon was far away from me. I was the fourth-tallest boy.

Captain Pratt pointed at the first boy and said an English word. Then he pointed to the second one and said another word. He pointed to the third boy, and then to me, and then to the boy after me, and so on. Every word was different, so I figured he was counting us in some white man way. He wrote something down on paper while White-Man's-Dog offended us by bluntly stating our Apache names.

The young boys were so sleepy they could hardly stand by the time four other whiteman-ized Indian students came in and started leading them away. I rushed to Orejon, but one big boy pulled me back to my spot while another took my cousin. Captain Pratt called a single word to the one with me, and he repeated it. It sounded something like "Dan-yell," but I had no idea what it might mean.

The whitemanized student motioned for me to follow him. He took me to a small room with three white-eyes sleeping pads propped up on short metal poles. Two of the pads already had a boy in them, making the sounds of sleep. Hopefully I checked their faces, but neither was Apache. The person said something to me in English, pointed to the empty pad, and closed the door.

I stood in the silence for many moments, trying to recover from the endless day's assault on my soul. I heard nothing in the darkness but the distant sound of someone crying softly. I knew it was a boy from my own beaten tribe.

I could not blame him. Like me, he had been robbed of his homeland, his family, his hair, his tribal clothes, and even his name. How could there be anything left of his honor?

As I walked toward the empty sleeping pad, I was surprised by the noise of my clunky, hard-leather, white-eyes shoes. I stopped and tried to take them off, but I could not understand how they had been tied on my feet and I could not see the tiny binding ropes in the darkness.

When I reached the pad, I pulled the woolen blankets off and arranged them on the floor, beneath the window. Refusing to use the sleeping pad was the only way left for me to protest my fate. *I would never sleep like the white-eyes!* I had only the tiniest shred of Apache pride left in what remained of my soul, and I refused to let my enemies steal it from me.

I worried about what was happening to the Chiricahua girls tonight and how my lonely cousin was doing without me. I longed to know if my mother was still ailing. I yearned to know if my uncle was still alive. I tried to pray to Yusn for all of my people, but it was so dark in my heart that he could not hear me. I could not seem to hear the prayers myself.

I patted my head, covered with stiff sprouts of hair shorter than the thorny spines of the pincushion cactus, and wondered who this broken, bald-headed, almost-warrior inside my skin might be. I felt naked without my breechcloth, yet I was covered from head to foot. I fought the odd, cloying pressure of the strange red flannel that now cloaked my body, the stiff, white-man collar of the bluecoat jacket jabbing at my throat, and the tension of musty trousers trapping my upper legs where a warrior's leaping muscles must be free.

I thought of White-Man's-Dog, and what had changed him into a whitemanized Apache. I vowed that no matter what happened, that was one thing I would *never* be.

I sat cross-legged on the rough white-eyes blankets and stared out the window, listening to the sound of the other boys, utter strangers, breathing in the dark. One persistently coughed. I did not want to wake them with my shameful sobs, but I lacked the strength to fight off the hopelessness and pain that choked my heart.

I did not sleep that night. I felt like a soft-skinned caterpillar building a cocoon to protect itself from the dangers of life among tarantulas and scorpions. With no help from Yusn, I said goodbye to my old life and armed my heart to fight the new one.

I was not yet ready to be a man, but by morning the last of my boyhood tears had dried.

CHAPTER

10

I STILL SAT ON THE WOODEN FLOOR when the other boys woke up at dawn. One of them—whose round face hinted that he might be one of the Zunis we had traded with back home—spoke to me in English. When I did not respond, he tried another tongue. I greeted him coolly in Apache, but he just shook his head. Finally he pointed to himself and said something that sounded like "Jon-a-than." Then he used his hands to show me that I was supposed to sleep on the "bed." He made it clear that tugging my blankets on the floor was something a "good white boy" would *not* do. This pleased me.

Another boy, long and lean, indicated that the white-eyes called him "Abraham." I knew the boys wanted me to tell them my name, but I had been trained not to do this, and there was no other Apache present to properly introduce me as "Solito." A few minutes later, White-Man's-Dog marched into the room and told me briefly that I would live with these boys—one Zuni, one Crow—who could only talk to each other, and to me, in English. He spoke to them as well. I did not understand what he said, but after that they always called me "Daniel."

I was hungry and hoped that we might be fed, so I silently followed White-Man's-Dog through some narrow wooden walls into a giant room, the size of a clearing where our band could put up camp. To my relief, I saw some other boys who had come with me, and some Apaches who had been stolen from Fort Marion earlier. They were hard to recognize without their hair.

On the other side of the room, I saw our girls. They had lost their beautiful long hair also. Their heads had not been shaved like ours, but their hair came only to their necks, white woman style, and they, too, wore white-eyes clothes that were all the same. Their long blue dresses made them look more like life-size dolls than strong Apache women.

Orejon was the last of our boys to arrive. He smiled at me bravely, but his big eyes could not mask his grief and fear. I edged over to him as soon as I could, hoping my strength would ease his terror, but he did not look relieved.

At once we were forced to march in lines to hard sitting places on long cut-trees-lying-on-their-sides. An old woman wearing a white apron patted all of us new Apaches from one spot to another until she was satisfied. White-Man's-Dog told us that we would sit together only until he had taught us how to behave in the eating place. Then we would be mixed up with boys from the other tribes so we would have no "temptation" to cling to our people or speak our native language.

Later, when Captain Pratt talked to us, I noticed that several of the students were coughing and could not seem to stop. We sat very still with our heads low while one of the older boys stood up and gave a serious English speech. As he finished, everyone said one long word together—"Aaaaamen"—and then we started eating.

I did not understand most of what went on in that room, but I did figure out what to do with the metal "plate" and "spoon." White-Man's-Dog taught us how to say these words in English and ordered us to repeat them. The younger boys did, but I remained silent. I refused to give the white-eyes or their dog the pleasure of hearing me speak their hateful tongue.

When we were done eating, we left the room in lines again. The other boys marched like soldiers. I refused. I walked slowly, alert for danger, as though I still wore moccasins instead of hard leather shoes.

I was surprised to see the outside of the school in daylight. Although there were many bluecoat buildings, there was a great deal of open space between them, and they pressed up against some low and very rugged hills. It did not look like home, but the variety of untamed trees and thick, green bushes told me that this would be a good place to hunt. I might even find some late-ripening berries up there. Anything I gathered myself would be better than the odd-tasting white-eyes food.

We headed out of the main fort building, across an open space, into another wooden building and up some stairs to a smaller room. This one had separate sitting benches for each of us, but each seat was attached to a tiny slab of pine that slanted toward the "chair." White-Man's-Dog pointed to an empty one in the back, and I stood by it reluctantly. No one sat down, so neither did I, until a young white woman entered.

She was puny, of course—all white women were—but to my surprise she smiled. It was the sort of smile that sweeps from the lips to the eyes by way of broad cheeks that fatten brightly. I studied her suspiciously, but I could see no evil there.

Still, I was cautious, and never risked looking at her face when she was watching me. Cheerfully she walked up to each of us new Apaches, held out her hand, and said something like "Welcometocarlislewhatsyourname?"

None of us knew what to do with her hand, but she took Orejon's and wagged it up and down in a curious way. After that the other boys followed, but I would not touch a white person, and simply looked away. I did not speak to her, and refused to respond when she called me "Daniel" several times during the day.

She held up things I had never seen and told us to repeat strange white-eyes words: "book," "paper," "pencil," and "globe." This last item looked something like the ball we used for playing shinny, only it was too large and too hard and had too many different colors on it. They were smeared together in such an odd way that I feared it was some sort of witch's tool.

When everyone finally rose to leave, I stood up, but this was the only thing I did with the others all morning. Miss Lawson—they all called her this, so I assumed it was her name—came to stand by me and spoke very softly, in a warm and friendly voice that made me suspect her even more. No white-eyes could be that kind, I knew. She must be a witch with some very dark plan in mind.

After the midday meal, I was taken to a big building, like a barn, heated by a huge burning pit where boys seemed to be melting tools. I could not understand what this place could be until I saw rows of the iron half-rings that white-eyes put on the feet of their horses. I had learned to track white-eyes horses from these rings many years ago, but I had never seen a white-eyes make one, or hammer it on to the hoof of the poor horse.

No one asked me to do much that afternoon, which was good, because I would have refused to do it. Some of the new boys brought wood to the fire but would not sweep the floor when they were told to. That was women's work, of course, and Yusn never intended for an Apache warrior, or even an Apache boy, to do the work he gave to girls.

After we left the place the whitemanized boys called "Blacksmith Shop," I followed them out to a big field. It was covered with grass that was, amazingly, all the same length, as though it had been close-cropped by sheep. The girls were at one end of the field wearing funny, shorter clothes and wiggling around in the same way at the same time. The boys changed their clothes to shorter things also, and this I did eagerly because I hated the itchy red "longjohns" and trousers. I wanted to wear anything that was more like a breechcloth and gave me room to move my legs. Besides, I hoped that if I got to go outside, perhaps I could have the chance to run. Not run away—I knew I could not do that yet. But to get back in condition for escape, I must run every day, following the training rules Uncle Angry had taught me.

But the boys did not run. They lined up again, sideways instead of front to back, and faced each other bent over like pairs of wrestling warriors. One of them had a piglet-sized funny fat ball that was pointed at each end. As soon as he threw it, all the other boys started to crash into each other. They jumped into piles as the weaker boys fell down! It was a ridiculous game with no purpose that I could see. How could knock-down-your-enemy-and-fall-on-him-ball possibly help a future warrior like me?

For the next few mornings, we went to Miss Lawson's class. We worked in our shops in the afternoon. Then one day we were taken to another sort of building. None of our regular teachers were there.

"The white-eyes call this Sunday School," White-Man's-Dog explained to us. "You will come here once a week and learn about Jesus."

One of the smaller boys asked, "What's that?"

White-Man's-Dog rolled his eyes impatiently. "Not what. *Who.* He is Yusn."

In Apache I asked, "Then why don't they call him that?"

I was astonished that the white-eyes were going to teach us about Giver-of-Life, and certain that they knew nothing about him that my family did not.

"Jesus is the white-eyes' Yusn," he told me. "He has many names besides Jesus—God, St. Nick, Christchild, Santa, and Holy Ghost."

We pulled back in mutual terror. A ghost! And White-Man's-Dog said his name out loud!

"His body breaks into three parts, and if you are good in the wintertime, he will bring you presents."

I knew this could not be true, and by the shifty way White-Man's-Dog delivered these words, I knew he did not believe it himself.

"Why do you tell your own people these lies?" I asked.

He glared at me. "I tell them what the white-eyes told me. They say we must believe in their Yusn to be saved."

"Saved from what?" I asked. "If this

Jesus-Ghost has evil white-eyes medicine, we need Yusn to save us from *him.*"

That night I slipped out the window of my room and climbed down a nearby maple tree to meet Orejon. I waited for nearly two hours before I spotted him awkwardly creeping toward me.

"You are sick," I whispered when he started coughing.

He shook his head. "I cannot be sick. There is no medicine man to cure me. If I get sick here I will die."

"Maybe," I suggested more gently, "you are only sick at heart. If we can hold a sack over your head four times, your loneliness will go away." This was a common cure for loneliness among our people.

"Yes," he said with some relief. "We do not need a medicine man for that."

But we did need a sack, so I promised that I would find one in the morning. Then I told Orejon that we needed to start collecting whatever we could—food, a water carrier, warm blankets, and a knife.

"It will take a while to plan our escape, but I will do it," I vowed. "We can hide things beneath this tree."

It was a majestic oak, encircled by big rocks covered with autumn leaves of rich orange and gold. I knew we should have found a small cave for storage, but I had to pick a spot on the school grounds. I could not conceal our cache in the traditional way.

"It will be hard to gather things in this awful place," Orejon complained. "They treat us like bluecoats. Everyone moves in lines. I cannot talk to the boys in my room. They do not speak our language. Why was there no room for me with our people?"

I swallowed hard. "My cousin," I said kindly, "I think there was room. They kept us apart on purpose. They want us to be Carlisle boys, not Apache men."

He coughed then, just the way my mother did, and I felt a sudden stab of fear that neither destiny awaited him.

CHAPTER 11

MY FIRST FEW WEEKS at the school were the worst in my life. I could not accept the food, the bed, the uniforms, and the bald head that had once held a lifetime of beautiful black hair. I could not get over the way I had been torn from my people. I ached for my mother, my aunt, my uncle, and the mountains that filled me with the spirit of Yusn. I could not bear the way the teachers, and even the other students—from twenty or more tribes—conspired to kill all the beliefs I held sacred.

And I was deeply worried about Orejon. When I got caught taking a torn old flour sack from the trash to use for my cousin's loneliness cure, I found myself in Captain Pratt's office, bent over for a whipping. I had been trained as a warrior, so the pain meant nothing to me. But the shame was unbearable; I had never been struck in this way before. Worse yet was the fact that I did not understand what I had done wrong. To my surprise, White-Man's-Dog found me alone that night and tried to explain it to me.

"The sack was thrown out," he whispered in our own tongue. "They do not say you stole it. They are upset because you wanted to use it for superstitious reasons, to hold on to the old Apache ways."

"My cousin misses his mother terribly and he's afraid his father is dead!" I protested. "If he feels better when I put a sack over his head four times, how does that hurt the white-eyes?"

"You must forget everything you have learned as an Apache," he said stoutly. "You must believe in the Jesus-Ghost and act in the Christian way."

A wild surge of anger gripped me. How could a Chiricahua ever say such things? I wanted to grab his neck and shake him. I wanted to bring him to the ground. "We named you right," I challenged him. "You really are the white man's dog!"

He glared at me, but the coward made no move in my direction.

"My name," he answered stiffly, "is Steven now."

At Carlisle, I hated the fact that I was surrounded by dozens of people all the time, but I had no one to talk to. Jonathan and Abraham, my roommates, had lived together for a long time and had become very close. When I refused to speak English to them, they gave up trying to be friendly. Most of the other Apache boys were as angry as I was, but they were afraid of being whipped for speaking our language, so they tried to speak English and kept a safe distance from me. Some of them still blamed Geronimo—and everyone who had ridden with him—for the trouble they were in. I tried to pretend I did not care, but I hated being pushed away from boys who had always been my friends. And some of them ignored Orejon, also, because he always defended me. Everyone but me now called him "Randy."

Within a few weeks at Carlisle, several of the Apache children had grown ill with the same symptoms that had stricken my mother at Fort Marion—coughing, weakness, struggling to breathe. It seemed that many boys and girls from the other tribes were sick, too. White-Man's-Dog told Orejon that when a student got very weak, the white-eyes sent him back to his family. Or so they said. All he knew for certain was that nobody ever saw them again.

While Orejon was thrilled at the possibility of being reunited with his mother and grandmother, even at Fort Marion, I was not at all sure that the white-eyes would truly send him there if he got much worse. I was afraid they would just kill him.

I was working on a plan of escape for us, but it still had a lot of holes. We had enough to eat, but not enough to hoard. We could not spare a blanket. We had no chance to make or steal weapons. All I could do was gather rocks the right size for bringing down doves, wood rats, and opossums. I didn't even have a buckskin pouch to carry them in when we began our journey.

I knew we had to start soon—before winter fell—but my cousin was still too sick to travel.

Each day I grew more worried that he might die before I could keep my promise to his father.

Although none of us were given warrior training, we all were trained to do whitemen's jobs. I learned that the boys who were not in the blacksmith's shop learned how to do other things—build white-eyes' houses, bake white-eyes' bread, make white-eyes' shoes. None of these forms of work sounded good to me. They were not the jobs Yusn gave to Apache men.

I had been at Carlisle several weeks when Yusn found another job for me. I was running around the great knock-down-your-enemy-and-fall-on-him-ball field, past the shop rooms, when a red-headed teacher I did not know happened to come out of one of the doors. Without slowing down, I glanced inside.

There were tools on the walls and stools on the ground, but this was true in all the shop rooms. What was special about this one was the sight of leather. Leather pieces, leather strips, leather scraps all over the tables and floor. As a child, I had once ridden on an Apache saddle made of leather! I had seen my uncle make reatas from strips of cowhide just like these! This was the first time since we had left our land that I had seen anything in the white man's world that reminded me of home.

And anything that might help me get there.

Ten days after I saw the horse-leather room, I stood at my desk one morning and waited for

Miss Lawson after she excused the rest of the class. In my head, I had practiced the English words I would need but had never said them out loud. Now, as she approached me, I found it even harder to talk to her than I had imagined.

"Daniel, may I help you?" she asked pleasantly.

For once I met her eyes and struggled to hide the hatred I felt for all her race. I still was not certain whether or not she was a witch, which made me feel guilty because she had always been so kind to me.

"Daniel?" she prodded. "Is something wrong? Is someone bothering you?"

I nodded slowly. Then I blurted out fast and awkwardly, "I want make saddle, harness in shop."

She blinked once, and I knew I had shocked her by saying that much. I waited for her to tell me I was "a good boy" for speaking English, but she didn't. She was silent for so long that I finally realized she had not been able to make out my words because my English was so awful.

I flushed and started to march away. But she caught me by the shoulder.

"Tell me again," she urged patiently. "What is this about a saddle?"

I fought back my pride and repeated more slowly, "I want make saddle. I want make harness. I hate blacksmith shop."

She nodded then, and smiled. "You want to be transferred from the blacksmith shop?"

"Harness. Make saddle," I said once more.

"You think you would rather be a harness maker."

"Yes," I said clearly. "Yes, yes, yes."

"Well, I'm certain that if you speak to the captain, he—"

"Captain, no," I snapped. "Captain worse than blacksmith shop."

She shook her head. "I'm so sorry you feel that way, Daniel. I know he can seem stern, but believe me, he only has his students' best interests at heart. If you explain to him—"

"Captain *no!*" I all but yelled at her. "You good. I ask you, Miss Lawson. You no help me?"

For the first time since I had met Miss Lawson, I saw sadness in her face. She did not know our ways, so she could not have understood what it meant when an Apache begged for help with a friend's personal name. But she heard the desperation in my voice, and to my surprise she said, "Of course I will help you, Daniel."

And she did. It took another week, a week in which I sat in her class and still pretended I could not speak a word of English, because I did not know whether to be grateful or mad at her for promising to help when she did nothing. But one afternoon, the white-eyes teacher I had seen at the harness-making shop came up to me as I left the midday meal and said, "Daniel, my name is Mr. Richardson. Today you are supposed to come with me."

I had been trained to show no feeling in

front of strangers, so I concealed my secret pleasure from him. But inside I felt a soaring hope not only because I would work with hides but because Miss Lawson had not turned out to be a witch. She really was my friend.

I rejoiced my first afternoon in the new shop. I paid attention to Mr. Richardson. If I understood him, I did what he said. If I didn't, I closely watched the other boys and imitated them. I learned that we were to start with the simple tasks of cutting leather, we were never to take knives or awls from the room, and we were not to touch Mr. Richardson's half-made saddle. But we swept up the scraps and threw them away, and to pick one up was not considered stealing.

By the time we went out to the field to play knock-down-your-enemy-and-fall-on-him-ball, I had already decided how I could show Miss Lawson my gratitude. At home we always brought food and blankets to our friends or family members, and captured ponies for them when we were able. I did not intend to steal horses here until Orejon was well and we were ready to run. But there was no way I could bring shame upon myself or my cousin by bringing fresh meat to a white-eyes.

I had no way of making a bow or arrows in the small room I shared with the whitemanized boys. I dared not steal a knife. But I could make a slingshot with the scrap of leather I had taken from the shop, and if that failed, I could sharpen a stick to spear some rats or moles.

CHAPTER ELEVEN

The next morning when we went into class, I stood straight and tall and waited for Miss Lawson. I watched her closely, feeling very pleased, as she walked in. She greeted us, and all of us—even I—replied, "Good morning, Miss Lawson."

And then she turned to lay a book on her desk. She did not look, but her smallest finger grazed the edge of one of the three rats I had left for her. They were scrawny things, not at all big and plump like our bushy-tailed wood rats back home. It had taken me quite a while to find three of them, but any less would not have made a full meal.

She pulled her hand back with the speed of a striking diamondback and swallowed a scream. All the boys leaned forward tensely, but no one spoke a word. They stared at each other in wonderment, and then they stared at me.

I didn't know how they figured out that I was the one who had left the rats, and I didn't know why they all looked startled. I had thought they liked this teacher. Hadn't any of them ever brought her a fresh kill?

She calmed herself and asked in a voice that was witch-hard, "Who is responsible for this?"

They all looked at me. I took a step forward. "I bring for you," I said, in English, to show her my gratitude.

She looked hurt and confused. And angry. I didn't know what to do.

"Take them out of here, Daniel!" she ordered

in a cold, dark voice I had never heard before. "Then go see the captain."

"Captain, no," I said to her.

"You go see him right now!"

I didn't know what had happened. Why had she helped me if she really did not like me at all? Had she just been waiting until I spoke English to prove she had conquered—or witched—me?

I took the rats and stormed off to the main building, steaming. I had spent half the night hunting down this fresh meat for Miss Lawson! How could she be so cruel as to send me to the captain? I did not mind the pain of the whipping that awaited me, but I dreaded the humiliation I would suffer once more at his hands.

And then, quite suddenly, I heard my uncle's voice, calling me from my soul, reminding me that he'd trained me to be a proud Apache warrior. I did not have to endure abuse from any white man! My job was to protect my family. I had to get my cousin back to his mother alive, and the longer I waited, the more impossible that obligation might be to fulfill.

I still carried the wood rats, so we had traveling food. I had hidden much of what we needed—certainly all we were likely to be able to collect at Carlisle. All we lacked were fast-moving horses. I could slip away and steal them now, then sneak back to our cache to meet Orejon when Moon came up tonight.

CHAPTER

12

I LEFT THE SCHOOL by way of a hole I dug beneath the fence and stayed hidden in a deep thicket all day. By twilight I was growing very thirsty, so I snuck through some nearby fields until I found a well not far from a white-eyes farmhouse. I stood behind a kindly oak for half an hour before I was certain that no one was about. Then I crept quickly up to the well, pulled up the bucket on the rope, and drank until my belly stuck out.

I had never actually stolen a horse, but I had listened to the warriors' stories all my life and helped out as a novice on three raids. As I crept through the abandoned fields of the farm with the well, I tried to remember the warpath words my uncle had taught me. To my shame, none came to me. I knew I should not touch my skin without the scratching stick, and I should only drink from Child-of-the-Water's tube. Then I remembered that only a beginning novice warrior had to do these things. All I had to do on my fourth raid was prove myself.

It was hard to think like a warrior while I was wearing the bluecoat uniform of Carlisle School. I was unarmed, and I could not run or jump with the ease I'd always known in a breechcloth and moccasins. And, of course, I had no Apache warcap on my half-bald head.

As full dark fell, I heard the nicker of a horse. At once I followed the sound, being careful to keep off the main road and out of sight.

I tracked the horse-noise to a large, weathered barn. I could hear a white-eyes voice, so I waited in the darkness until a young girl came out of the building carrying a bucket of the thick, white liquid that white-eyes loved and Apaches despised. There were oil lamps burning in the nearby farmhouse, and the sound of laughter once she went inside. I was so hungry I was sure it was time for the white-eyes to eat their dinner. I thought it was safe to take my shoes and stockings off and creep silently into the barn.

The heavy wooden door creaked mightily. I froze, afraid the white-eyes people might have heard me, but no one came. I stood still as my eyes adjusted to the night. To my right I saw a black and white cow. Beyond her were two old horses, the big kind, good for pulling wagons but short on speed. All of the animals were chomping contentedly. They did not seem at all alarmed at the sight of a stranger.

I looked around and found a white-eyes rope and tied it loosely around the black horse's neck. I led him from his stall and kept him close to me. I went to the dun-colored horse and tugged him away from his hay by his mane. Then I reached up one foot, braced my toes hard against his leg, and swung myself onto his broad back. I pressed hard with my heels and knees and pulled on the rope until the black horse followed. Both animals looked longingly at their dinner, but they were well-trained and did not fight me.

As we slinked from the barn through a dry, fallow field, my heart thumped terribly with fear . . . and then with newfound pride. I had done it! Completed my fourth raid! And with no man to help me! What a glorious start to my return to the land of Yusn! Orejon would be heading home protected by a *real* warrior now.

I imagined Uncle Angry's face, and I hoped he was alive to hear my story. I could see my mother serving me sumac berries and roasted elk as I sat proudly in front of my own fire. As a warrior, I was free to have my own wickiup, my own voice at council, even my own wife. Not that I wanted one, yet, but still, it was—

Abruptly, the black horse whinnied. I did not know why. And I should have known! I should have been paying attention to every tiny sight and sound, just as Uncle Angry had taught me. Instead I was patting myself on the back before the job was done.

Beyond us, another horse whickered. Then both of my horses called to the other one. Desperately I hoped that it was a wild horse, or one in a pasture, or one carrying some disinterested passerby.

But I was still close enough to the barn to

be on the owner's land. My heart clutched when I heard a white-eyes call, "Coralee? Why are the horses out?"

He was close. I could not see him, but his voice almost echoed off the nearby hickories. For a moment I froze, not certain whether it would be better to risk the noise of a quick escape or hide and hope he would ride right on by me. Uncle Angry would have known.

The loud man's mount neighed again, and mine cheerfully answered him. A moment later I could hear his horse trotting toward the one I rode. I pulled on the black's rope and dug my heels into the dun's flanks, wordlessly commanding it to run.

In a heartbeat the man was after me. It was too dark for him to see, but he surely knew his horses' voices and could tell they were not where they should be. He also knew—and I did, too—that he was riding a fast, young saddle horse while I was trying to escape on two heavy draft animals with all the speed of contrary mules.

The dun's "gallop" was barely a lope. The black horse only jogged. Frantically I let go of the black's lead and tried to escape with just one horse. After all, I was fit and strong and could run forever. It was my sick cousin who had to have transportation.

Behind me, I heard the man talking to the black, which was dragging the rope behind him. By now he surely realized that the horse had been stolen.

CHAPTER TWELVE

"Stop!" he hollered, his mount once more running full speed after me. "Stop, you horsethief, or I'll shoot you in the head!"

I was not quite certain what the English words meant, but I knew I was in trouble, even before I heard a bullet whizz by my throat.

I knew I could not ride fast enough to escape him. But he didn't really want me. He wanted his horses. Maybe I could escape if I abandoned the dun, too.

I leaped off on a slight rise that was sparsely covered with thin trees and scrawny bushes. It was nothing like the wonderfully rough country Yusn had given us to escape our enemies, but it was all I had.

My plan worked. For two minutes. Maybe three. But the dun stopped running as soon as he realized he had no rider, and the man caught up with him almost at once.

Then he came gunning for me.

It was a brief struggle, and I lost. If it hadn't been for Orejon, I might have risked my life for freedom. But my duty to my family came before my pride. There was still a chance I could help my cousin as long as I was alive.

The farmer ordered me to walk in front of him, rifle at my back, for at least three miles, maybe four, on a gravelly road that led past several farms. It was very hard because, with his rope hobbling my ankles, I had only half of my normal stride. By the time we reached a nearby town, I had rope burns on my wrists. Stickers, burrs, and cuts lined the bottoms of my feet. I was an Apache; I could endure pain. The fear and shame I had to battle.

There was no one to open the jail door when we arrived, but the farmer banged on it until a sleepy-looking fellow with a star on his shirt finally appeared. I did not understand much of what he said to the farmer or what the farmer said to him. But after Star-Shirt hauled me roughly into an iron-barred cell, I had no difficulty interpreting the slam of the door as he locked me in.

CHAPTER 13

IN THE MORNING, Star-Shirt brought me a thin, tasteless soup and asked me some English questions. I was not sure what he said, and I saw no reason to answer. Even if I spoke his language, I knew he would not understand why I had stolen the horses. He would look at my "crime" in the white-eyes way. He could not see that it was an honorable Apache thing to do.

It was only my capture that shamed me. Looking back, I realized that I had made many novice errors. The horses were draft animals, big and slow. I should have passed them by and looked for faster mounts. And once I heard the farmer coming, I should have abandoned the raid and slipped away! I know my uncle could have escaped without detection.

I spent many hours trying to sneak out of my cell, but the iron bars were well set. As the day dragged on, I found it hard to cling to my hope and pride. By late afternoon, all my confidence had vanished.

Then, abruptly, I heard rapid hoofbeats and the slamming of the front door to the jail.

Five minutes later I recognized the sound of hardsoled shoes. I clung to the bars and vowed to conceal my terror. When my turn came to die, I would prove I had the strength of a warrior.

Still, my heart was pounding as Star-Shirt stomped toward me waving a giant key. And it almost stopped when Captain Pratt barged into view.

I cringed, waiting for him to yell at me, to whip me, to tell me I had disgraced him and every fine student at Carlisle. He was furious; I could see it in his eyes.

But his voice trembled with another emotion as he asked at once, "Did they hurt you, son?"

Shamed by his concern, I merely shook my head and looked away. But when Star-Shirt opened the cell door, Captain Pratt marched in and took my wrists in his big, strong hands.

"There are rope burns on this boy!" he protested.

"He was like that when he came in. You couldn't expect the farmer who caught him stealing his horses to just ask him nicely to follow him to jail."

Captain Pratt glanced down at my swollen bare feet. "Why did you take his shoes?"

Star-Shirt shook his head. "He didn't have any when he got here."

The captain turned back to me. "Did the farmer take them?"

I could not meet his eyes. "No. White-eyes shoes make noise."

He took a deep breath. "Then you are guilty of stealing the horses?"

My arms grew stiff. I could not answer. I was mad at Captain Pratt for all he'd done—I had stolen the horses partly to escape from Carlisle before another whipping?—but now I owed him, too.

He leaned down until we stood almost face to face. "Why did you do it?" he whispered.

I told him the truth. "My cousin very sick. Must have horse to reach his mother so we can all go home."

The captain did not reply. He just spoke quickly to Star-Shirt before he led me from the cell.

No freedom came without a price, I knew, but I did not understand the full cost of my rescue until we returned to Carlisle. I rode in behind the captain on the back of his horse, in full view of all the students, who pressed against their windows to stare at me.

I turned my head. I was humiliated by the fact that I had utterly failed to carry out my first solo raid and, worse yet, that I had needed a white-eyes to rescue me.

My frustration grew even worse when the captain took me into his office and called in White-Man's-Dog. White-Man's-Dog wore a shining clean uniform. Mine smelled of horses and the jail.

The captain sat down at his desk, while I

stood before him stiffly. I understood some of his words. I certainly understood that he was angry.

"You have disgraced the school," White-Man's-Dog translated. "You have broken the law like a common criminal. If the captain had not vouched for you, you could have been hung or spent years in prison."

I studied the ground, fuming.

"He has been patient with you. He knows it is hard to adjust to a new way of life. But this is the only way of life left to you. The Chiricahua land has been taken. The tribe has been locked up. Your cousin is too ill to go running off at the start of winter. You must bury your dreams of escape. Either you become a good white boy, or you will end up an outlaw.

"The captain gave the sheriff his word that you were too new here to understand the white-eyes' laws," White-Man's-Dog continued. "He promised to make you pay for your crime by working extra hours every day. He says that if the horses had not been returned or anyone was killed or injured, there would have been nothing he could do for you."

I did not move.

"He wants to make certain you understand that if you defy his orders, or the orders of any teacher here, or try to stir up trouble among the other boys, he will take you back to the sheriff. If you break any other laws, he will not protect you. If you do not try to learn English and learn the white-eyes ways, there will be no hope for you."

At last, I nodded. Inside, I would still be Apache, and I would let none of the white-eyes ways stain my heart. But now I must learn everything I could about my enemies and pretend to obey them. It would help me to escape the next time I tried.

"The captain wants your word that you will not dishonor him."

My eyes flashed up to meet Captain Pratt's, hard and piercing. To my surprise, I saw a ghost of kindness there. I reminded myself that he had saved me, and I had not even called his name. I would have owed him a tremendous debt if he had been an Apache.

Finally I said in English, "I will obey."

When I got back to my room, the other two boys were studying. They did not greet me. It was early yet, but after all I had been through, I was very tired. I took off my dirty uniform and, without pulling the blankets onto the floor, crawled into my white-eyes bed for the first time. It was amazingly soft.

In the morning, I hurried to the eating room so I could speak to Orejon, but he was not there. I had no pride left to swallow, so I turned at once to White-Man's-Dog.

"Where is my cousin?" I asked in Apache.

White-Man's-Dog said, "I have been told to speak to you in English."

I was so angry I almost hit him, but I knew nothing good would come of a fight at Carlisle, even if I won. I had to know what had happened to Uncle Angry's son.

"Where is Orejon?" I asked, in English this time.

"Who?"

He knew perfectly well who I meant! He wanted to make me use Orejon's English name.

"Where is Randy?" I spit out, so furious I could hardly form the words.

"Randy is in the infirmary. He got quite sick after he stood up to Miss Lawson for you the day you ran away."

"What happened?"

"After you left, he told Miss Lawson that bringing fresh meat to a friend is the Apache way to say thank-you. He told her that roasted rats are good food. She realized she had made a mistake. She sent him after you. He ran all the way to the captain's office, hoping to catch you before you did something stupid." He paused for a moment to let his point sink in. "He was too late."

I didn't want to go into that. "So why did they put him in the infirmary?"

"Because one of the cooks found him lying in the hallway on the floor by the captain's office, coughing so hard he could not stand. He has tried to hide how sick he was from all of us, but now he cannot."

Guilt slithered through me. I would have stood up and rushed to my cousin, but I knew that White-Man's-Dog had been told to watch my every move. I must sit here and eat. I must go to class. I must go to the harness-making shop. I must do extra work as punishment for my failed raid. Somehow, I would have to find a time—and a way—to see Orejon without breaking the promise I had made.

When I arrived at Miss Lawson's class, she greeted me along with the others as though it were an ordinary day. I had never answered her before, but now I did the best I could, stumbling over the English words that the other new arrivals had long since mastered. Miss Lawson did not comment on the sudden change in my efforts to learn English, but when class was over, she asked me to stay.

She stood at her desk, distant, almost afraid. "I am sorry I failed to understand the nature of your gift to me, Daniel," she said apologetically. "I told the captain that everything that happened afterward might have been my fault. I told him that I truly thought you had had a change of attitude once he agreed to put you in the harness-making shop. It took a while, but he finally agreed to give you a second chance."

I did not speak. She sounded as nice as ever, but I knew now she was a witch.

"If you want to come with me, I can get you into the infirmary for a few minutes before lunch," she added almost conspiratorially. "But you can't stay very long."

My throat grew tight with reluctant gratitude.

"Daniel, do you understand me?" she asked.

"Yes, Miss Lawson," I said stiffly.

She wanted me to forgive her, but I could not.

The infirmary looked like a giant bedroom, full of children I had not seen in a while. Orejon had been given a bed near a window that overlooked the grassy field, but he lay quite still, with his eyes closed. As I crept to his side, he began to cough. I was relieved to see proof he was still alive.

"Oh, cousin, you are all right!" he greeted me in Apache, grabbing my hand as though he were a little boy. "I knew you would not leave me, so I was afraid something terrible had happened when you did not come back."

"I had some trouble getting you a horse," I answered in our native tongue, hoping Miss Lawson would not tell me I must speak in English. "But Captain Pratt made everything all right."

Orejon looked startled. "Do what he says," he pleaded. "I could not bear it if they took you away."

I stood beside him, not sure what to say. "Are they taking care of you?"

He didn't answer that. "I feel so bad," he whispered. "I am afraid."

That made me scared, too. We had been trained never to complain of petty troubles or insignificant fears. I knew he understood how serious his situation must be.

"What can I do?" I asked, leaning down

so he could whisper something that might be against the rules.

To my surprise, he answered, "If I die, tell my people that I never forgot I was an Apache."

And then he cried.

CHAPTER 14

It was cold that winter, but I did not mind it, because I welcomed the snow. It reminded me of home. I knew that Yusn had given us winter so we would have water in the springtime, when sometimes the Arizona mountain snowpack melted so fast we had to run straight up hills to escape the mighty flash floods. I wondered how Scarred-by-a-Woman was doing at home . . . if he had even made it back there. I knew he could not survive the coldest months without a wickiup, but he had no woman to make one. I had never heard of an Apache man building one before.

The white-eyes talked less about the snow than about their upcoming midwinter ceremony. One day Miss Lawson explained that "Christmas" was the holiest time of the year for the white-eyes, when they celebrated the birth of their Giver-of-Life. She told us that we must respect this special baby, who wasn't really a baby, but a grown man and then a god. I tried once to tell her about Yusn, but she said I must forget my Apache god and only worship hers. I was so offended that I did not speak to her for days.

CHAPTER FOURTEEN

There was one thing I liked very much about Christmas, and that was the home-like smell of pine. For some reason that I did not understand, Captain Pratt ordered a magnificent long-needled pine brought to the hall near the eating room. When no one was looking, I gently stroked its branches.

The next day some whitemanized Indian students embarrassed the stately tree by covering it with funny looking toys and candles. They did other strange things as Christmas approached. They slid down snowy hills on flat pieces of hickory, screaming as they went. They walked very fast on long, skinny pieces of wood hooked to their snowboots, using iron poles to stay upright. There was a frozen lake near the school and sometimes when we went there the boys and girls wore funny knife-soled shoes to glide around it. I never understood such silliness.

Even stranger were the winter "socials" they held at the school. The white-eyes trained the boys to speak to the girls in a certain way, to touch their arms to lead them to a chair, and to dance in a certain way around the room. I was appalled. No decent Apache girl would let a boy touch her, and when she did need to speak to him, she would always turn away. It hurt me to see so many of our girls giving up the old ways. They already dressed like white-eyes. Did they have to act like them, too?

I did not have time for such games. Captain Pratt had assigned me two hours of extra work at the stables every afternoon. Miss Lawson had arranged a special time for me to go see Orejon each day and tell him winter Coyote Tales as we had done back home. He always seemed glad to see me, but his rattling cough grew worse and worse. Despite my prayers to Yusn, I saw no sign that he was gaining strength. I tried not to let him see how afraid I was for him.

Miss Lawson helped me write a letter to my aunt explaining that Orejon was ill. She said that all the children did this and the interpreters shared the words with their parents. I had little faith in this form of communication, but there was no other way to send the message. I also wrote a letter to my mother, asking her about her health. Miss Lawson said she did not know what might have happened to Uncle Angry and Cougar-Feet, but she would try to find out for me.

To show Miss Lawson I was grateful, I did my best to learn what she tried to teach me. I soon realized that it was not enough just to be able to speak English and understand it. I also had to look at odd squiggly marks on paper and translate them into English. We had no such writing system in Apache. But since childhood I had been taught to read the smallest signs in the mountains—a broken twig, a fall of leaves, the press of a moccasin or cowboy's boot heel into soft soil. I pretended that the paper marks were the footprints of cactus wrens and scrub jays, and this helped me quite a bit. I could read a few words clumsily by Christmas.

One day, everyone grew very excited when

we approached the eating room and found small colored packages under the pine tree. We all got to open one. Mine had new white-eyes stockings. I noticed that there was nothing there for the students in the infirmary, so I took my stockings to Orejon.

He coughed a lot, and spoke to me in a very weak voice. He asked me to tell him another Coyote Tale, so I picked the one about how Coyote was fooled by Rock Rabbit. It had always been his favorite.

My cousin was asleep before I finished. I sat there watching him for some time, then squeezed his hand and begged Yusn to help him.

When I returned to my own room, Jonathan, the Zuni, told me that Miss Lawson had come to see me and had left me a Christmas gift. I was astonished and pleased until I saw what it was. Mud! Tiny blocks of mud! My ears reddened. Had she fooled me again? Was she once again bewitching me?

Then Abraham, the Crow, said, "Fudge! I wish she'd made some for me. May I have a piece?"

I was shocked. I handed him the small container and watched him put a square of mud in his mouth. His eyes rolled and he licked his lips. Was he teasing?

I was too worried about Orejon to play games, but at last my curiosity got the better of me. I took a very tiny piece and laid it on my tongue, but I did not chew it.

It did not taste like mud. It was sweet,

taunting . . . delicious! I could not believe that white-eyes food could ever taste like that!

Jonathan laughed when I offered him a piece. "You should have seen your face when you first saw the fudge, Daniel. It was the way Miss Lawson looked when you brought her the wood rats."

"But even white-eyes know what rats are!" I protested.

He shook his head. "White-eyes don't eat rats. They think they are dirty and disgusting . . . like eating mud."

For the first time I understood what had happened the day I ran away and I thought Miss Lawson had betrayed me. I knew it was time to forgive her for her ignorance of Apache ways. In spite of the way I had treated her, she had always been good to me.

I ended up giving most of the fudge to my roommates because it felt so good to have them speak to me, even if it was in English. The next morning I was eager to go to Miss Lawson. I thought it would be wiser to thank her outright than to risk bringing her another gift.

It turned out that I did not have to wait until class to see my teacher. I found her waiting for me in the eating room at the break of day. I was in a happy mood and tried to thank her for the fudge, but she ignored my words and told me to follow her.

I feared I had done something wrong again, but I could not think of what it might be. I had tried so hard to keep my promise to Captain Pratt, to keep all my hatred and frustration locked up inside.

When we had reached a quiet corner, Miss Lawson turned to face me. To my surprise, I saw tears in her eyes. When she tenderly touched my arm, it frightened me.

"I checked on your cousin this morning, Daniel," she whispered in a voice that trembled with honest pain. "I am so very sorry to tell you that . . . last night . . . he passed away."

There was no way I could deal with the death of He-Who-Was-My-Cousin. A thousand feelings, all of them awful, exploded inside me and would not go away. My hair was still cut very short, but I hacked off a piece in the front to honor him with mourning.

To my horror, they nailed He-Who-Was-My-Cousin's body in a box and carried it away. They would not let me burn his belongings, and he had no horse for me to kill. My friends from my free months with Geronimo's renegade band, and others from the reservation, treated me kindly, but they were all careful where I was concerned. I had caused so much trouble that they were afraid to be seen with me.

I could not even run outside in the winter because of the deep snow. I would not tie stupid knife-blades to my shoes or long wooden sticks as the others did. Sometimes I ran in circles in the barn just to stretch my legs. I knew Uncle

Angry would be ashamed of how weak my body—and my spirit—had become. Far worse was the fact that I had utterly failed to achieve the only thing he'd ever asked of me. I'd left the women alone and I'd let his only son die.

I went crazy thinking about it, so I kept busy any way I could. When I could not go outside, I worked at learning to read. In February I discovered newspapers and realized that there was a way to find out more about what was happening to my people. The government was still discussing where to send them, since there were dying quickly at Fort Marion. The business people in Florida wanted to keep them because the tourists came to town. Another tribe in North Carolina was discussing offering them land. The government wanted to send them to another white-eyes prison in Alabama. My people wanted to go back home to the land of Yusn, but the white-eyes in Arizona said they would kill them if they did.

Miss Lawson showed me how to read maps of these different places, and I was thrilled to see a map of home. I told her the names of the mountains and the springs where we had lived so happily, and she showed me where she had grown up—in Vermont—and told me that a special man she knew there had asked her to come back home. I learned that it was not so rare for a young white-eyes woman to go somewhere without her family, and that she might pick a husband without the consent of her father and his. I still found it hard to understand the ways of white-eyes, especially white-eyes girls.

By the Moon of The-Leaf-Buds-Are-Swelling, the students got to play on grass again, and this time I recognized the sport of bluecoat-ball. I missed the games of shinny and hoop-and-pole that I had always played with He-Who-Was-My-Cousin and my friends. One day when Jonathan and Abraham were talking about how much fun "baseball" was, I decided that I should learn to play.

I was good at running, but they had to teach me what it meant to "slide into second base." I thought it made much more sense to throw myself at the second baseman and bring him down, but the other boys insisted that I must skid along the ground on one foot and rise up like a striking rattler. This way the second baseman could not reach me.

I had no trouble throwing the ball; that was like throwing stones at ground squirrels. What I didn't understand was why I was supposed to toss it to a player on base to stop a runner when it would be faster to just hit the runner in the back with the ball. And I did not understand, when I got to be the pitcher, why the boy at home plate kept moving the bat around. How was I supposed to hit the long wooden stick with the ball when he did that?

Finally, Jonathan offered to be catcher and told me just to throw the ball at the fat glove on his hand. He moved it up and down a few inches every time I pitched. I never understood exactly why, but if I threw the ball right to his mitt, the boy with the bat always frowned and the boys on my team cheered. For me!

I felt good about my first bluecoat-ball game, good about my tiny step toward being accepted by the Carlisle boys. But it was a short moment of pleasure, because on the way back to my room a small Cheyenne girl ran up to me and told me to report at once to Captain Pratt.

CHAPTER 15

"SIT DOWN, DANIEL," Captain Pratt said to me.

I sat uneasily on the stiff wooden chair. I was still in my bluecoat-ball clothes. There was dirt on my chest and grass stains on my knees. I had assumed that playing with the other boys was something that would make the captain happy, but I must have made a mistake for him to be angry with me.

"I saw you pitching out there today," he started casually. "You've got quite an arm."

I shrugged. "A boy cannot eat if he cannot throw," I told him, "unless he eats only what his father kills for him."

I was trying to be modest in the face of praise, as I had been taught, but when his lips pulled down, I could not think of anything safe to say.

"You don't have to kill for your food now, Daniel."

"No," I agreed.

"No, *sir,*" he corrected me.

"No, sir," I said stiffly. It was hard to hide my anger. I had worked so hard to keep my bargain, to keep from dishonoring him! Was there nothing I could do to please this man?

"Miss Lawson tells me you have made a great deal of progress on your reading."

"She is a good teacher," I said, hoping that was safe.

"And Mr. Richardson? Is he a good teacher, too?"

I tried to think of what I could have done wrong in the harness-making shop, but nothing came to mind. I did not like Mr. Richardson as much as I liked Miss Lawson, but I had caused him no trouble and he had been fair with me. More than once he had said he was pleased with my progress.

"I have tried to do what he told me," I told Captain Pratt. "I am sorry if I have displeased him."

The captain stood up and walked around his desk until he stood beside me. I did not look up.

"Why do you think you have displeased him, Daniel? What have you done?"

I tried not to show him how much I hated being called the white-eyes name he'd given me. "I do not believe I have done anything wrong, Captain," I said truthfully. "But I have made you angry when I thought that before."

He heaved a great sigh and went back to his chair. For a moment, the room was silent.

"Do you understand how hard I worked to start this school, Daniel?" he asked me. "Do you have any idea how many people told me it wouldn't work? That I could not teach 'savages'?

That Indian children were 'too stupid and lazy' to learn?"

My eyes flashed up at him. I knew he did not agree with such white-eyes' lies, yet it still hurt me to hear him repeat them.

"But I always knew that all you children needed was a chance. Especially you, Daniel. You came here with so much anger, but also with fire and courage and love for your people. I never meant to hurt you. All I wanted to do was to kill the Indian inside you to save the whole man."

I was too outraged to speak. How could he care for us—and I knew by now that he did—and honestly believe such an ugly thing? If he killed the Apache boy in my soul, there would be no more *me*.

With a warrior's self-control, I said, "I promised not to dishonor you, Captain. I never promised to agree."

He sighed again, then turned to stare out the window. I could hear a giant clock ticking behind me. I could hear the horses asking for their supper. The sound of footsteps filled the hallway before he turned back to me.

"Daniel, many of our students go to families for the summer to learn farming skills. You have had more trouble settling in than most, and I am not certain that you are ready to leave our supervision. But Mr. Richardson says you do splendid work in the harness-making shop and are ready to serve as an assistant to a skilled man."

I did not answer. To agree would be boastful. To argue would be rude.

"I have received an application for an outing student from an elderly Quaker who lives on a small farm but makes most of his living mending local harnesses. This might be the perfect summer place for you, Daniel, but only if you think you are ready."

"Ready?" I asked. "Does Mr. Richardson think I am prepared?"

The captain stared at me. "I'm not speaking of your skills as a harness maker, Daniel. I'm speaking of your . . . willingness to leave your Apache anger behind."

I had been trained not to lie. I did not want to stay at the school when all my friends would be gone for the summer—even the two teachers I had come to like—and I liked the idea of going to a farm where I could work with leather. But my "Apache anger" was far from dead. As long as I lived it would not die.

Everything would be ruined if I said so.

Carefully I said, "I have learned how to behave like a good white boy. I can do it for the summer."

He touched my chin and made me look him in the eye.

"Do I have your word?"

"Yes," I said stiffly.

"Yes, *sir*," he corrected me.

"Yes, *sir!*" I repeated, but I burned inside.

CHAPTER FIFTEEN

A few weeks later I boarded yet another train and headed away from the setting sun, but more than that I did not know. Some of the Commanche boys who had been at the school for two or three years took the train alone to their summer places, but many of us rode together with Mr. Richardson. This train was terribly hot, as the others had been, but with the windows open I felt more at ease, and in my school uniform, at least I could stay neat and clean. This time the noise did not frighten me, and I knew how to sit in the train seats with my feet on the floor. We were not locked in one train car like convicts this time but mixed with the white passengers and treated like people.

Almost every time the train stopped, someone would speak to Mr. Richardson and then take away one of my schoolmates. Five of us finally got off together. I was proud that I could read the sign above the platform. It said "Welcome to Downingville, Pennsylvania."

A group of men, dressed in overalls and baggy shirts, walked toward us hesitantly. Mr. Richardson greeted them warmly before he matched us up to our summer "fathers."

Mine was the oldest of the group. He had short, white hair around the bottom of his head but nothing in the middle. At first I thought he might have been scalped, but there was no puckered line or sign of damage.

He was thin and fairly tall—at least, taller than I was—and he wore small round spectacles which I had learned were designed to help people see. His skin was brown, not the brown of birth but the brown of a lifetime spent working in the sun. He did not smile but his blue eyes showed no darkness as he held out his hand to me.

I knew what to do this time, and I took his hand politely, trying not to grimace as I touched his skin.

At home I would not have asked a stranger's name nor given one, but Miss Lawson had taught me what to do.

"They call me Daniel," I said, but the last word sat bitterly on my tongue.

The old man's name was Orville Hamilton, he told me on the ride to his farm. I sat beside him on the bouncing wooden seat of a battered farm wagon pulled by two overgrown horses called Daisy and Rose. He spoke to them gently, as though they were old friends.

"What did they tell thee about us, Daniel?" Mr. Hamilton asked me.

I had never heard this word "thee" before, but Miss Lawson had warned me that Quakers used some funny talk. They also believed that the Jesus-Ghost meant for them to be kind to Indians.

"They told me to work hard for you and be courteous always," I answered stiffly.

He glanced at me, then looked away. "I bought this land just before I got married, almost sixty years ago. It took me a long time to save the money, but my dear Annie waited for me. It's hard to wait for things when thee are young, but thee will find that it's worth working for."

"Yes, sir," I said when he stopped talking.

"I was apprenticed to a harness maker when I was only ten, Daniel. Trained for seven years before I earned my freedom. I loved the work but hated the man." He glanced at me again and, to my surprise, winked at me. "Don't tell my wife I said that. We're Quakers and not supposed to hate anybody. But it's hard to be young and strong and have an old man treat thee like rocky soil."

"Yes, *sir,*" I repeated, with feeling this time.

He smiled at me, his blue eyes alight. "Does thee speak English, Daniel, or is 'yes, sir' all thee knows how to say?"

"I speak English," I said bluntly, without a hint of warmth. "I gave my word to the captain I would be courteous. I am speaking to you as I have been taught."

He whoaed the horses, then turned to face me. A long moment passed before he began to speak. "Son," he said softly, "I can only guess what thee has suffered. My wife and I, we won't try to change thee. We know what it's like to be different from other folks and have them not understand. All we want to do is give thee a home for the summer so it won't be so hard being away from thy own parents. Courtesy is a good thing—I admire it and demand it in my house—but we don't want thee to be afraid to breathe for fear thee will anger us. We want thee to feel at home."

There were many things I could have said. But he was white, so I didn't dare believe that maybe he was a decent man. I had made a vow to Captain Pratt and I meant to keep it. I wanted no more trouble until the right time came for my escape.

"Yes, sir," was all I said.

I loved Mr. Hamilton's farm. It was not large but it grew thick with vegetables—green beans and tomatoes and long-eared corn—and sported proud fruit trees of many different kinds. Long before we reached the house and barn, I spotted willows and cottonwoods, dozens of them, tall and draped in leaves. I knew a stream must be near. As we got closer I could hear the water. My heart smiled. This was a place I could come to and talk to Yusn, a place to mourn and plan and dream.

"The harness shop is on the back side of the barn," Mr. Hamilton said as we pulled up to the house and jumped down from the wagon seat. A big brown dog, half-deaf and white-muzzled with age, dragged himself to his feet with a wildly wagging tail. His joy was clearly for Mr. Hamilton. With some caution, he sniffed at me.

"This is Roscoe," Mr. Hamilton told me. Then he said to the dog, "This is Daniel. He's all right. Be nice to him."

The dog seemed to understand. I held out

my hand and he licked it. He even wagged his tail once or twice for me.

Mr. Hamilton said, "My Annie will want to meet thee while I unhitch the team."

I knew I was supposed to volunteer to help, but I thought it might be rude to tell a stranger I would handle his stock. I had ridden horses all of my life, and I had been making harness parts for almost eight months. Because of the extra work Captain Pratt had assigned me in the stable, I also knew how to hitch and unhitch a working team.

"I will help you whenever you wish," I said cautiously.

The old man looked tired. "I know thee will."

Before I could say "yes, sir" again, an old woman hurried out of the house, rubbing her hands on her long apron. She wore an ankle-length black dress and a funny white covering on her head. Her snowy hair was pulled back in a serviceable bun and smile-wrinkles covered her face. She was a tiny thing and fluttered around like a finch.

"Daniel?" she sang out, as though she had known me for years. "It's so good to have thee with us!"

To my astonishment, she threw both scrawny arms around my shoulders. I did not move. I dared not touch her.

"Good afternoon, Mrs. Hamilton," I said formally when she finally released me.

"Oh no, only strangers call me Mrs. Hamilton," she corrected me. "It's plain old Annie to friends and family. And since thee has come to live with us, Daniel, now that means thee."

CHAPTER 16

EVERY DAY of the first month I spent with the Hamiltons, I found myself grateful that Captain Pratt had trusted me enough to send me to them. I did not know how white-eyes boys lived, but I knew that Annie and Orville truly meant to treat me like family when they let me sleep in a room that they said had once belonged to their two sons. I had never slept alone before—except in jail—and the knowledge made me feel both free and lonely.

The room had a big, wide window that opened to fresh air and many rich-leaved trees. The bed was big enough for two or three people, with a beautiful blanket made of many small square pieces stitched together, all soft and colorful. The floor was covered with some sort of thick blanketish thing as well.

I did not spend much time in the room because I was busy working in Orville's harness shop. It was not very large and not very clean, but he knew where every tool hung on the wall. He also knew the background of every man who brought him a harness to be mended, and the family of every man who asked for a new one to be made. He worked on saddles rarely, but the ones I saw him make were splendid. If I learned half of what he knew, I was sure to become an expert in my trade.

Orville treated me as a partner more than a servant, right from the start. He never gave me orders; he just made suggestions. He corrected me when I made a mistake, but he did not try to shame me. When I did things right, he was quick to offer praise. It made me feel guilty that I had hidden a knife and a rawhide traveling pouch in my new getaway cache near the creek, but I had been taught never to take chances, never to trust a white-eyes. No matter how kind the Hamiltons seemed, I was still an Apache who had been trained to always have a backup plan.

Shortly after I arrived for the summer, I discovered that many days the local Quaker ladies came to worship with Annie. Most of them were kind to me, although one of them did not seem certain whether or not it was safe to have a Indian work at the farm. I was always tempted to sneak up on her in warpaint, but I resisted the urge.

They met in Annie's living room, not in a church, and whenever I forgot and came inside during their meetings, they did not seem to have a lot to say. Once I asked Annie about this, and she told me that Quakers did not have to make noise to pray. Sometimes, she said, "Thee must be still to feel the Light."

I did not understand her faith, but I felt that in this way, it might be close to mine. Apaches did not believe in talking when feelings could be better shared without words. And it had always been in silence that I had heard Yusn speak to me.

One day, a new lady arrived for the worship hour with a white girl about my age. The girl was driving the carriage because the old one was somewhat crippled. Roscoe roused himself from a nap on the porch to greet her with a happy bark and a wagging tail.

"Martha! I'm so glad thee could join us," Annie greeted the smiling woman.

"I've missed thee," Martha said. "I was afraid I would never get well."

It was steaming hot, even under the trees, and I did not need Annie to tell me to take the matched grays to water in the shade. I was not surprised when she introduced me to her neighbor and her granddaughter, Polly.

But when Polly followed the horses toward the barn, I was shocked.

"Have you been here long, Daniel?" the white girl said to me.

I could not believe it! An Apache girl would die before she would speak up like that to a boy she had just met, let alone follow him to a place where there were no older women. I was so tense I could hardly let go of the harness leather. I would be blamed for this, I knew.

"No," I said, hoping that one word would

be polite but not encouraging.

"Are you one of those Indian boys from Carlisle?"

"Yes." I wrapped the lead reins around the hitching post and walked away.

By the time I reached the harness shop, she had caught up with me.

"What tribe are you from?"

I felt my chin rise. "I am a Chiricahua Apache," I replied, unable to stifle my pride.

"Oh, how exciting!" she gushed. "Tell me what it's like to be an Indian."

I turned. I stared at her. She was not only going to get me into trouble, she was going to be rude.

"What is it like to be a nosy white girl?"

Her face flamed. It was a pretty face, I noticed, nicely oval and set off by thick, black curls.

"I was only trying to be friendly." She licked her lips. "Most of the Hamiltons' neighbors are old, and I thought you might be lonely for some friends your own age."

She turned then, and would have flounced away except, for some reason, I stopped her.

"I did not mean to hurt your feelings," I said truthfully. "But I . . . I have a job to do here, and I cannot afford to get into any kind of trouble."

She took a step back toward me and asked, "How can I get you in trouble?"

I was the one who flushed as I answered, "You are a girl."

CHAPTER SIXTEEN

The next week the summer "outing agent" arrived from Carlisle School to check on me. He was supposed to come once a month. I knew that if I was very unhappy, or if the Hamiltons were displeased, he would take me back to school with him.

Annie served him coffee and a slice of her wonderful apricot pie. After he had eaten every bit and they had talked about the weather, the agent said to Orville, "Would it be better to speak to you and your wife without the boy?"

Orville glanced at the agent, then at me. "If Daniel wishes to speak to thee privately, that is of course his own affair. But there is certainly no reason to keep him from hearing anything thee has to say to my wife and me. Surely you understand, sir, that we consider Daniel family."

After that, I began to relax at the Hamiltons. I stopped saying "yes, sir" all the time, though Orville would say it to me sometimes when he meant to tease. When he took me into town to pick up supplies, he introduced me to everyone he knew, making it clear that he trusted me to conduct his business. I was honored by his faith in me, but after my experience in jail, I was uneasy going into a white-eyes town alone.

One day, in early July, Orville asked me to hitch up the team so he could drive to the train depot to collect his daughter. Ruth, he told me, was married now and lived with her husband and children in a state called New Jersey. The whole family came to visit twice a year—every summer and at Christmastime.

Orville went to town alone while I helped Annie set up tables for a "potluck" meal outside the house. Apparently all the neighbors in the area came to eat at the Hamiltons' for a celebration whenever Ruth came home. Ruth's husband also had family nearby, as well as many friends.

Some of the neighbors got there before Orville did, and Annie cheerfully introduced me to each of them. Over and over again, they said the same thoughtless things.

"So you're from Carlisle Indian School!"

"What's it like to be an Apache?"

"Did you really ride with Geronimo?"

I was relieved when Orville drove up with a wagon full of happy people. For a while, nobody bothered me. This was just as well, because when I saw Ruth's husband, George, greet Annie, I could hardly keep from lecturing him. He put his arms around her and gave her a kiss on the cheek! Then he talked to her, right to her face, and made no effort at all to turn his back to her! No Apache son-in-law would ever have shown such blatant disrespect to his wife's mother, whom he was never supposed to talk to, never supposed to see. He was required to leave the wickiup whenever she entered. This man had not even brought his own tent!

But no one seemed to be disturbed by George's rudeness except for me. Once again I realized how little I knew about the white-eyes and their mysterious ways. Ruth and George were polite to me, but showed me no special interest at first. Harry, their five-year-old son, seemed excited that his grandparents had taken in "a real-live, honest-to-God Indian." Their baby, a little girl, seemed too young to notice there was anything different about me.

I knew some of the white people who came to eat, and of course I had to be polite to them. The ladies from the worship hour all showed up. I remembered their names, but I was not rude enough to use them. Polly also bounced up to greet me. I nodded courteously when she said hello, then slipped away before she could pester me.

I was not able to escape from the throng of white-eyes, though, because Annie insisted that I sit beside her so she could whisper the names of people and strange white-eyes foods to me.

Everyone was so happy that I felt very lonely. This was the sort of family gathering I had once loved back in the Chiricahua Mountains. I wondered what sort of rejoicing my mother and aunt could have with my uncle in jail and He-Who-Was-My-Cousin gone to The Happy Place. I'm sure they worried constantly about what was happening to me.

As I remembered our family life together—the tribal drum pounding, all the feet dancing, the bloody meat dripping over the fire—I had the strangest feeling that I would feel out of place celebrating Apache-style now. Was it because I was ashamed to face my uncle? Because I still grieved so much for He-Who-Was-My-Cousin? Because I had never finished my final raid?

Or was it because I had been taught to live

the white-eyes way? I relished Annie's home-cooked food and ate it with a knife and fork. I had learned to enjoy the softness of a white-eyes bed. I didn't even spend much time thinking about the itchy longjohns anymore.

The realization scared me.

Little Harry, sitting by my side, did not let me forget about my people. He peppered me with questions about my other life all through the meal. He wanted to know about riding horses bareback, shooting arrows, and leaping on white settlers out of trees. I tried to concentrate on using my utensils, but he was hard to ignore.

"Did you ever go into battle against our soldiers?" he asked.

"Not exactly," I answered honestly. "But there were times when they were close."

"You mean, they were after you?" He was breathless with excitement. "How many did you kill?"

As his high, young voice rang out across the table, the noisy conversation came to a clumsy halt. I didn't know what to say.

The truth? *I never killed one, but I prayed constantly to Yusn to give me the chance.*

The lie Annie's friends would want to hear? *Of course not. Only bad Apaches shot at soldiers, but I was always a good one.*

The silence was crushing while I searched for the right words to say. Finally I stammered, "We surrendered before I had proven myself as a warrior."

I could almost hear a sigh of relief around the table. Desperate to escape the boy, I glanced as far away from him as I could—and to my astonishment, spotted something I had never seen before. Two identical little girls.

I knew what they were at once, though I had never seen twins before. Twins were taboo for Apaches. It was not possible for both to grow up, so one always died at birth in the mountains. Sometimes I had heard hints that the father's mother helped the weaker one to die, but no one talked about this, especially to a boy. As I watched the two girls laughing, I felt as though I were seeing ghosts. And ghosts were serious trouble for Apaches.

"What do you have to do to become a warrior?" Harry pressed. "Kill someone?"

Before I could think of an answer that would not horribly embarrass Annie, Polly stood up and walked around the table to my side.

Just what I need, I thought miserably. *Another white-eyes asking me stupid questions.*

Polly said, "Daniel, would you come with me for a second? I need you to look at my bridle."

It seemed like an odd request in the middle of a meal, but I was so grateful to escape from Harry that I excused myself, as I had been taught, and quickly followed her.

Polly said nothing more until we reached the huge walnut tree under which her horse had been tied.

Before I could touch the bridle, she said,

"There's nothing wrong with it, Daniel. I just thought you needed some help getting away."

I turned to stare at her, astonished that she had seen so clearly what I had been going through.

Before I could speak, she said, "I know you don't want to talk to me anymore than you want to talk to Harry, so I'll leave you alone. After our last talk, I promised myself I wouldn't bother you."

I felt a curious blend of relief and shame as she flounced away. And then, belatedly, a touch of gratitude.

CHAPTER

17

THE NEXT DAY I ASKED Orville how white girls were supposed to act and whether it was safe for me to speak to one. He told me that he knew I was a gentleman, and as long as I treated each white girl as a lady, I would have no problems.

I wasn't sure just what that meant, but the next time Polly came to the house, I tried to act nicer. Over the summer she came many times, chattering away while I cut leather and milked the cow. I learned many things from her. She was the one who told me that the Hamiltons' two sons had died years ago in the War-When-the-White-People-Fought-Each-Other. Quakers, she said, did not believe in war, but one of the boys had helped northern soldiers as a doctor and another had been killed by a slavecatcher while he was leading a group of dark-skinned people to freedom. Polly said that the loss had hurt Annie and Orville so deeply that they rarely spoke of either son, and it was one reason they were so eager to do their best for me.

Polly also told me that Orville sometimes had pains in his chest, and Annie was very worried about his condition. I admitted that I was worried about my own mother's health, and I was not yet certain that my uncle was still living.

Polly, of course, wanted to know everything about my past. I did not want to talk as much as she did, but eventually I told her I was born in the White Mountains, probably to the White Mountain Apache tribe, and would have died if my mother had not adopted me. I explained that she had lost her own husband and three children to the bluecoats before that time, so I had never had a father.

"So you're not really a Chiricahua?" she badgered me. "You're some other kind of Apache?"

I pondered that a moment. "In my heart, I am a Chiricahua. When we lived on the Fort Apache Reservation—not too far from where I was found—I thought about trying to find the mother who gave me birth. But my own mother—my adopted mother—would never let me talk about it. My uncle said I must do nothing to hurt her."

"I understand," said Polly. "Still, it must be strange not to know how you ended up alone as a tiny baby."

I had wondered about it for years. "Many Apaches were in battle with the bluecoats then. I think maybe someone tried to hide me from the soldiers."

"And couldn't come back?"

I nodded. It was the only explanation that had ever made sense to me. Of course, it did not account for why I had not yet been cleaned or blessed when my mother found me, why I had not been wrapped in the proper blanket or buckskin.

To change the subject, I asked Polly why she did not use "thee" and "thy" like the Hamiltons. She told me that the Quakers were changing just like the rest of the country, and some were pressing forward to be like other Americans and some were clinging to the past. I told her that I thought the same thing was happening to some Apaches.

Most of our conversations were peaceful times, but one day Polly brought news that alarmed me. She said that a burglar had attacked two farms, stealing the life-savings of some elderly local farmers. I did not have much use for money and told her so, but she explained that white-eyes must have money to eat and live.

I knew this already. Carlisle School made Orville keep a special account for my earnings that I could have only with Captain Pratt's permission. But Orville did not believe in banks, and he and Annie kept all their cash hidden in a big cookie jar in the kitchen. The Hamiltons were close to Polly's parents, but I didn't think I should reveal the cookie jar secret to anyone.

It no longer surprised me that I felt such loyalty to Orville and Annie. They had treated me as a member of the family right from the beginning, and I was finally starting to feel like one.

It was the middle of August when the outing agent came back to check on me again. I had been doing very good work and had avoided any problems when I went into town, so I was certain that no trouble awaited me. In fact, I was wondering how I could go about asking the agent or the Hamiltons if I could come back here next summer, or maybe not return to the school this fall.

The agent gazed hungrily in the direction of Annie's kitchen, and she laughed as she brought him a piece of homemade pie, fresh peach this time. He didn't stay long because he could tell that all was well and we were happy. He almost forgot to give me a letter as he said goodbye.

"I don't know what it is, Daniel," he told me cheerfully. "Captain Pratt just said I should deliver it since you won't be coming back for a few weeks. It's from Vermont, if that's any help to you."

I did not know the names of all the white-eyes states, but I did know that one. Miss Lawson had gone there for the summer. I was pleased beyond words that my teacher cared enough to write to me.

"Would thee share thy letter with us, Daniel?" Annie asked pleasantly. "I've never had a chance to hear thee read."

I knew that what she really wanted was

to be handy in case I needed help. I was determined to prove I could read the letter by myself.

" 'My dear Daniel,' " I begun smugly, proud of what I could do. " 'I hope you are doing well this summer. I have gone home to Vermont, as I told you, but I will not be coming back as I had expected to.' "

I stared at the letter for a moment. Miss Lawson was not coming back to Carlisle? Disappointment balled in my throat.

" 'The man I once mentioned to you has asked me to marry him. It is very hard for me to give up teaching all my wonderful students, but I believe this is the right thing for me to do.' "

My voice was slowing down now, and I suspect Annie thought I was having trouble reading. She moved closer and leaned over my shoulder as I continued.

" 'You know how proud I am of all you've achieved, Daniel, and how much I will miss you. I could not leave my position without carrying out the promise I made to you. I have sent many letters regarding your family and finally, with the help of an influential friend of my husband-to-be, received the information you requested.' "

I began to tremble. If my people were well, wouldn't she just say so?

" 'Your uncle Angry-He-Spears-Bluecoats is alive. He has been moved to Mount Vernon Barracks near Mobile, Alabama. Your aunt and grandmother have recently joined him. So have your cousin, Makes-a-Good-Home, and her baby. I am told that your family was properly informed of your cousin's sad passing.' "

I closed my eyes in relief . . . and fear. Uncle Angry still lived, but Miss Lawson had not mentioned my mother . . . or Makes-a-Good-Home's husband.

Annie read the words out loud, because my voice had broken.

" 'I do wish I could send you only good news. But life is not always what we hope it will be. Some months ago, Cougar-Feet was shot and killed trying to escape, and I am told that your dear mother passed on shortly before your tribe was moved from Fort Marion. . . .' "

I did not wait to hear the rest of the letter. Something in me snapped. I could not stay in this white-eyes house, listening to a white-eyes read about the death of my loved ones at white-eyes' hands. I desperately needed to grieve with an Apache.

But there was no one for me. I ran to my secret getaway cache. It was still sparse. In addition to my knife and rawhide pouch, I'd collected some dried meat, a white-eyes tin of water, an old blanket, a slingshot, and a spear I had made shortly after I arrived. It was all that remained of the world of She-Who-Was-My-Mother. All that remained of the Apache Way my uncle had once taught He-Who-Was-My-Cousin and me.

I could not cry, but I could scream. And I screamed my rage at the white-eyes, all white-eyes, who had stolen my land and destroyed my people and taken my whole family away from me. I remembered everything about our life together, and everything about our time apart. I remembered the bluecoats who had chased me, the reservation agents who had cheated on our rations, the doctors who had not saved He-Who-Was-My-Cousin or the beloved old woman who had rescued me and brought me up. I went black with hatred and red with rage. I emptied what was left of my soul all afternoon and evening, and I was still there, pounding on the ring of rocks that sheltered my cache, when the sun came up.

The first ribbons of daylight reminded me that it was my job to milk the cow. With a shock I realized that I had forgotten to do the barn chores last night. I had also failed to make Orville's deliveries and run his errands. I had run out on Annie.

I knew Captain Pratt would drag me back to Carlisle when he heard what I had done. He had sent me to the best family in the world for my summer outing, but I failed to conquer my "Apache anger," just as he had feared.

Why should I stay here and face his fury this time? I suddenly wondered. *No one knows where I am. I could just take off with what I have hidden.*

Scarred-by-a-Woman had jumped off the train with less.

But he had been certain where he was

heading, and I had no place to go. How could I run to She-Who-Was-My-Mother if she no longer lived? How could I face my uncle and aunt when I had failed to save their son? How could I run two thousand miles to home alone and what would I do if I ever got there?

I was too numb to think, too numb to care. I could find no solution. There was nothing to do but go back to the Hamiltons' barn and milk the cow.

I walked back so slowly that the black-and-brown rooster was still crowing when I got there. No one was stirring, but I could hear the sound of voices coming from Annie's beloved kitchen. Then the porch door banged open, and Orville trudged down the back steps, carrying the empty milk pail.

I stood ten yards or more away, but I could not meet his eyes. "I am sorry," I said in a voice so low I was not sure he could hear me.

He did not answer. Instead he hollered, "Annie, he's back!" He dropped the pail and rushed in my direction.

Instinctively I ducked. I had never seen Orville move so fast.

But when he reached me, I saw no anger on his wrinkled face. His eyes were red and his eyelids bagged. He wrapped his trembling arms around my shoulders and drew me to him as though I were a lost child.

"Thank thee, Lord, for bringing our boy home safely," he whispered as he pressed me to his chest.

Suddenly Annie was there beside him, hugging both of us and weeping. "Orville told me I should not go after thee, that thee needed thy own time to grieve. But when thee did not come back last night I was so afraid!"

I was too moved to speak. To my surprise, my arms slipped around the two of them, and I held on tight.

Orville milked the cow, as he had the night before, while Annie filled me up with eggs and toast and dumplings. She did not ask about my feelings, or my plans. She just let her love wash over me, peeling away layers of my pain and hate.

After Orville returned, we all sat around the kitchen table in companionable silence. When the time seemed right, I started talking, slowly at first, uncertain if I should, but too much in need to stop myself. I told them everything: how I had been accidentally abandoned at birth and rescued; how I had come almost to the brink of manhood with Geronimo's renegade band; how I had tried to honor Miss Lawson with rats and been caught stealing the horses; how Captain Pratt had saved me and I had tried to be good but He-Who-Was-My-Cousin had died anyway.

I told them about my promise to my uncle, who was like a father to me, and my shame that I had utterly failed to live up to his expectations. I told them the absolute truth: I could never be a white-eyes and did not want to be, but I saw no way for anyone to be a true Apache anymore.

When I was done, Annie said nothing. She just took my hand.

Orville leaned back in his chair and rubbed his left shoulder, as he did sometimes when he was very tired. Then he said thoughtfully, "I'm getting too old to run the shop by myself, Daniel. I need somebody in the family to take over. I think we should speak to Captain Pratt about having thee continue with thy studies in the fall right here at Polly's school."

CHAPTER 18

OF COURSE IT WASN'T AS EASY as that. I had to go back to Carlisle to see Captain Pratt, listen to his lectures, and make new promises to "be good." He seemed happy that I was doing so well with the Hamiltons, but he made it clear that I was still *his* student, and if I had any trouble, I would have to come back to Carlisle.

I rode Orville's favorite bay every day to the new white-eyes school. I felt so different than I had my first few weeks at Carlisle! I hadn't arrived in a breechcloth and moccasins this time, and my hair was as short as everybody else's. I still struggled with some peculiar white-eyes customs, but at least I spoke English and understood what most of the students said. I didn't hate everyone.

Polly introduced me to all of her friends as "Daniel Hamilton." They weren't quite sure what to do with me, but they tried to follow Polly's lead. I was grateful to have a real friend again, even if she was a girl.

When Christmas came this year, I knew what to expect. The Hamiltons' daughter and her family came to stay with us again. I did my best to avoid little Harry, especially when anyone else was around to hear his questions. Ruth, I noticed, did not speak to me very much but watched me almost constantly. I got the feeling that she was afraid I would do something "Indian" to her father and mother.

For Christmas, Harry gave me a wallet made of snakeskin. I could hardly bear to touch the thing—Apaches never, *ever* handled snakes—and it was hard to say the words I had been taught to show my "gratitude." I threw it away the moment I was alone in the barn.

Once Harry asked why I called the Hamiltons "Orville" and "Annie" instead of Grandma and Grandpa as he did. I told him that when we first met, they had asked me to call them by their first names. That night, Annie took me aside and said, "Daniel, we are family now. In our hearts, you know we have adopted you. I would love for you to call me Grandma."

I didn't know what to say. I was honored, in a sense, but shamed by the sudden image of my uncle's face. How would he feel if I called a white-eyes by a kinship name? Wasn't it bad enough that I had totally failed to hold his family together? That I had let He-Who-Was-My-Cousin die? The grief of my losses still ate at me daily, but it was nothing compared to my shame.

Annie said no more about it, but it hurt me when I realized later that she did not smile for the rest of the day.

Ruth cried when she left on New Year's Day

and she begged Annie and Orville to come visit her soon. She assured me that I was welcome, too. But we all knew that Orville could not go anywhere unless I was there to look after the farm, and none of us were sure that leaving me alone was a good idea. When the locals met me on the streets, some still averted their eyes or seized their daughters' hands more tightly. There was still a burglar raiding neighboring farms, and though nobody ever said so out loud, we all knew that some folks in town blamed me. After all, there were no suspects, and I was an Indian, which was proof enough. The Downingville sheriff even came to the farm once to "warn" Annie and Orville about the ongoing night attacks of the burglar, but the look on his face made it clear that he had really come to see if they were safe with me.

As the winter passed, we fell into a comfortable routine. I now did more harness work than Orville, and he made sure that I was the one who made our trips to town, first with him and then by myself as people got used to me. Once he rode in alone for an appointment with the doctor because his heart was giving him increasing pain at night. After that I never let him pick up anything heavy and I kept a very close eye on him.

At night we sat before the hearth, and Annie would read to us from the Bible. Once, when I was quiet for a long while, she asked me what was wrong. I admitted that I missed the winter nights my people had spent around the wickiup fire, telling Coyote Tales and our own story of "In the Beginning." She wanted to hear more, so I told her about White-Painted Woman, Lightning and Child-of-the-Water, and how we had carried their stories from one generation to another for centuries without needing pen or paper. I knew that she and Orville did not believe in Apache ways, but they listened very attentively. From that time on, they would ask me to tell an Apache story after the Bible reading. I was very pleased that they wanted to listen, and pleased that after all my time away from my people, the stories still came back to me.

Annie started leaving books in my room on all kinds of subjects—old Greek myths, Bible stories, rowdy western adventures, big-city mysteries, even poetry. I liked some better than others, but I loved being able to read when it was too dark and cold to do much outside. My mind would take me where my legs could not go. The more I pretended I was somewhere exciting, the less I thought about all I'd lost.

I continued to go to the white-eyes school, except when the snow was too deep, and I was content most of the time. Some of the students, I think, stopped thinking of me as "The Indian" and treated me as another boy named Daniel. I never told them my real name was Solito, and I never tried to tell anyone but Polly and the Hamiltons how I felt about my home. I was not close to any of the boys my age, but when spring came I asked if I could play bluecoat-ball with them.

CHAPTER EIGHTEEN

At first I had to be very careful not to hurt the other players. They had not been trained in Apache-style wrestling, and when I jumped for the ball my temptation was to knock a boy down and pin him to the ground. But I remembered what I had learned about the game at Carlisle, and I soon impressed them all with my speed at sliding into bases and my pitching skill. One day I struck out every hitter on the other team, and my teammates for the day were so happy that they all jumped on top of me. For once it felt good to be crushed by a group of white-eyes.

I hurried home to tell Annie and Orville about my very happy day, but when I reach the farm, I could not find either one. When I called, no one answered. I could hear the cow bawling loudly to be milked, and the horses neighed when they saw me coming, rushing over to the corner of the pasture where they were always fed. Roscoe did not greet me. He was always dozing on the porch when I came home from school, but today he was nowhere to be found.

I knew Orville would want me to see to the stock, but first I had to find out what was wrong. Too many times I heard stories of Apache men coming back to their camps to find the women and children and old ones butchered by bluecoats or Mexican troops. I felt the same sick fear that I knew my uncle had known then.

"Annie?" I called out, rushing into the house. "Annie, where are you?"

I searched every room but saw no sign of

her. I even knocked on Annie and Orville's bedroom door, something I never did, and finally opened it to be sure no one was sick in there.

Smoke was filtering through the house. I was afraid something was on fire, but all I found was an untended pot on Annie's stove. What was inside might have started out as soup, but it was too burned to for anyone to eat—even an Apache on the run.

I flew out the back door and ran to the barn. The animals looked hungry, but uninjured. Finally I heard Roscoe whimpering, pawing at the door to the shop behind the back stalls.

I took a deep breath and pushed the door open, terrified of what I might find.

I almost smacked the door into Annie. She was kneeling on her heels, bent over, sobbing, but alive.

My relief lived only a second before it died.

On the ground before her lay Orville, splayed out on his belly, arms askew, one leg flung out in a way that was not natural for a sleeping man. Annie had edged close enough to rest his head in her lap, and she never stopped stroking his face as she cried.

I had seen death enough times to know that Orville's time had ended. But I had never before felt grief for a white-eyes, never even imagined that the death of one would not be a cause to rejoice. Now it was as though my heart slipped out of me, as though it were Uncle Angry who had died.

Apaches do not fear death, but we do fear the dead, especially their ghosts when they come back to visit. I did not want to stay near this body, or touch it, or stay in this shop which Annie surely would not burn. But Annie, crouched on the ground before me, looked helpless and broken. I could not leave her. When she met my eyes, I felt as though she were the child and I the strong man.

Annie took her husband's hand—already losing warmth—and rocked back and forth as she kept on weeping. I sat down beside her and pressed her head to my chest. She clung to me and sobbed for half an hour without ceasing.

At last it grew dark and she grew quiet.

I touched her face, so wet and red, and she turned to face me with timeless grief in her ancient blue eyes. Hoping Yusn would understand, I straightened Orville's body and lay his hands on his chest in a matter more dignified to face the Quaker Happy Place.

Then I helped Annie to her feet and said gently, "Grandmother, it is time to come inside."

CHAPTER 19

THE NEXT FEW DAYS were very hard for Annie, and very hard for me. I did not know what to say to her, and I was afraid that she expected words of comfort and would think I did not care because I could not say them.

The house was full of her friends, white-eyes who knew me but did not understand how I felt. They thought I was just the hired boy, an Indian no less, on loan to the Hamiltons for a while from Carlisle School. They did not know that I, too, had lost a loved one.

I stayed away from all of them as best I could, doing everything He-Who-Was-My-Grandfather had taught me. I milked the cow twice a day and fed the horses, giving each enough exercise to keep fit. I kept the barn and workshop sparkling clean—cleaner than He-Who-Was-My-Grandfather had ever kept either one. I had been trained by my uncle to memorize sights or facts in an instant, so I rarely needed to check the list of orders and repairs that He-Who-Was-My-Grandfather had shown me. I started to work on them at once.

Apaches did not hold big funerals the way white-eyes do, but I knew that Annie would want me to attend her husband's. I had written to Ruth the morning after Annie had found him sprawled out in the workshop, but she lived a long way away and we had not heard from her yet. I had planned to take my grandmother to the graveyard the day of the funeral, but Polly's parents hoisted her into their carriage and drove off while I was in the barn. I did not know what to do.

Unhappily I saddled up the bay and followed on my own. If He-Who-Was-My-Grandfather were an Apache, I would be preparing to kill his favorite horse for him to ride in The Happy Place. Once it had seemed right to me—the only right thing to do. Now I knew it would grieve Annie, and He-Who-Was-My-Grandfather's spirit, so it would be wrong. I was torn between my two worlds, as always, but relieved that the bay could keep on living. After all, he was my friend, too.

I did not want to watch them bury He-Who-Was-My-Grandfather's box in the ground, but I dismounted and stood by the bay to show him honor. I prayed to Yusn to take care of his soul in the white-eyes way, which seemed strange to me, even though I was beginning to believe that Yusn, in some strange way, was also the white-eyes' God. I knew that Uncle Angry would never understand how I could pray for a white man or feel such pain at his loss. But my uncle had taught me to stand by my people, which meant I could not leave He-Who-Was-My-Grandfather's spirit or Annie herself alone.

As I stood at a safe distance, I glanced at my grandmother across the tiny graveyard. She looked almost blinded by her pain. I wanted to go to her, to take her home, but I dared not interfere with the white-eyes ceremony which she found sacred. I did not want to interrupt or cause her any shame.

Suddenly Polly was at my elbow. I felt a moment's peace that a white friend had chosen to stand by me.

"Daniel, Annie is waiting for you to join her. She asked me to tell you she will visit with her friends later. She needs her family now."

It took me a moment to realize that the only relative Annie had at the funeral was me.

A few days later, Ruth showed up alone with the children because her husband could not "get away." I did not understand this. Uncle Angry would never have sent my aunt alone to deal with the death of her father.

At first I was glad to see them. It was difficult to run the shop and farm, go to school, and take care of Grandmother Annie, too. She still cried a lot, and she needed someone to sit with her, to listen, to nod and say "I remember." But I wanted to hold my memories of He-Who-Was-My-Grandfather inside. It was not the Apache way to speak casually about the dead.

After Ruth had stayed with us two weeks, I began to realize that she was afraid to go home. One afternoon while Harry and the baby were sleeping, she came out to the barn to talk to me.

CHAPTER NINETEEN

I was picking out the bay's hooves since he'd just brought me back from school, and I wasn't sure whether I should stop and listen or keep on working. I didn't think Ruth would stay very long. There was nowhere for her to sit.

"What are your plans, Daniel?" she asked abruptly. "I mean, now that there's no one here to train you in the harness-making trade."

I leaned against the bay's ribs and pulled his foreleg back between my knees. As I scraped out his hoof, I was careful not to meet Ruth's eyes. I knew a white-eyes trap when I heard one. "Your father was an excellent teacher," I told her. "I am lucky that he gave me so much time."

She seemed to understand that I had dodged her question. "Yes, I'm sure you've learned a lot here. But now that things have changed, I'm wondering if you might be better off at Carlisle."

There it was. As blunt as it could be. I swallowed my anger. "I will do whatever my grandmother asks of me."

I turned back to the horse, but Ruth laid her white hand on my shoulder.

"Daniel, she's very fond of you, but she's *not* your grandmother," she said softly. "She's deep in grief, and right now she can't bear the thought of leaving here. But in time, I know you'll move on and then she'll be alone. And you can see she's getting old. I think she would be better off selling the farm now and coming back to New Jersey to live with me."

In time, I know you'll move on. I did not know what to say. I had come to think of this farm as my home. Besides, where else could I go? Unless General Miles kept his promise to someday free my people and return them to Arizona, it made no sense for me to join them in prison—even if I could bear to face Uncle Angry. I did not want to go to our beloved Chiricahua Mountains, or even the Fort Apache Reservation, all alone. I might have some birth family there, and now that She-Who-Was-Mother was gone, it would not hurt her for me to seek them. Still, I loved Grandmother Annie, and she needed me. I was making a life here. I had no intention of letting another white-eyes rip my life wide open.

There were many things I could have said, but respect for Grandmother Annie stilled my tongue.

After that, Ruth was cool to me until she left for New Jersey. Grandmother Annie was still in shock and said very little. Sometimes she kept busy around the house, but other times she would forget to cook. Then I would swallow my pride and do women's work, clumsily fixing something to keep her strong and also enough to feed me.

Grandmother Annie had not asked me about the harness shop, or the business books He-Who-Was-My-Grandfather had taught me to keep. As far as I knew, she was still using the kitchen cookie jar for household funds, and carelessly took out cash in the presence of friends. I knew I would have to add to her money soon to keep her safe and comfortable. Although I had kept all of our deadlines and done good work, He-Who-Was-My-Grandfather had extended credit to many people, and I was afraid they might not feel they owed this payment to me.

Most of our customers asked me about Grandmother Annie and were quick to pay because of concern for her. But some of them clearly thought an Indian boy had no business living with an elderly widow, let alone trying to manage her finances. I think they were afraid I would steal from her . . . or lift her scalp.

One day I tried to deliver a magnificent new carriage harness and encountered the hard reality I could expect if I tried to make my way alone in the white-eyes world.

I hitched up the team and carefully laid the harness in the wagon on top of an old quilt. I made sure none of the edges rubbed against the wood. I dusted off the leather one more time and made sure that all the silver buckles and bolts were shiny before I started on my way.

I reached Mr. Anderson's grocery shop in the forenoon. Since a man was helping a white-eyes lady carry some things out to her wagon, I waited by the door until he was finished. When he walked right by me without a glance, I followed him inside.

I had gone no more than four or five steps when he turned around and barked, "You, boy, get out of here. If you want something, you ask at the back."

I knew that my people were treated this way at home, but most of the white-eyes I had met in Pennsylvania had not acted like this, especially when I was with the Hamiltons. Locally, Grandmother Annie and He-Who-Was-My-Grandfather were very well respected, and some of that respect had been passed on to me.

I almost turned around and left, but then I remembered that I had done fine leatherwork and deserved to be treated the same as any other Pennsylvania craftsman. He-Who-Was-My-Grandfather had told me that I must never allow his customers to push me around because I was an Apache.

"I have a delivery to make to Mr. Anderson," I said calmly.

"Oh, you do, do you," the white-eyes sarcastically replied. "Well, Mr. Anderson is getting married tomorrow and took off early today to tie up some loose ends. I'm his uncle, and as long as I'm filling in, no redskin is going to barge into this shop without my say-so."

I stood my ground. "Mr. Anderson needs this harness for his wedding. He specifically asked me to bring it here today."

He glared at me. "We take deliveries *in the back*," he insisted coldly.

As he turned and marched off, I called out, "Excuse me, sir, but there's the matter of the fee."

He spun on his heel, his face red and gleaming. "Surely you don't think I'm going to turn over my nephew's cash to an Indian!"

My lips grew so stiff I could hardly speak the white-eyes tongue. "Mr. Anderson agreed to pay me on delivery." I did not add that I knew my grandmother needed the money to pay for a fresh load of hay.

"I knew Orville Hamilton for forty years!" the old man bellowed. "He was supposed to make that harness! Not some half-grown savage!"

I felt a granite shell of anger encircle me. I realized that if I left here feeling beaten, I would never be a man. I was in the right. I had done good work, delivered the harness on time, and stayed polite in the face of hateful arrogance. I must win this battle on white-eyes terms.

"If I don't receive payment for the harness, I will take it back to the shop, and your nephew can make other arrangements to collect it."

"Why, you little—"

He swung at me, and would have found his mark, if I had not ducked. It was instinctive, a gift from the years of training by my uncle. It was a miracle I held back and did not use my knife on him. I stopped only because I knew too well how the law worked when an Apache clashed with a white-eyes. It didn't matter who had started it. The Apache always paid.

I took a step back. I clenched my fists and

tried to hold my ground. "Mr. Anderson can come out to collect the harness if he chooses. Otherwise I'll sell it to someone else. You can explain to him why you refused delivery."

This time I was the one who turned to go. I kept my head high and my eyes hard, refusing to reveal my shame. I took my time, checking the sparkling new harness in the wagon and the old one on the team. Then I got up in the spring seat and clucked the horses to be on their way.

Only then did he stop me. He took two steps out the door and held out an envelope marked "Uncle Edward: Please give this to Daniel Hamilton when he brings the harness." The old man did not even speak to me. He looked angry enough to spit in my face.

I took the envelope, opened it to be sure that nothing was missing, then slipped it inside my shirt. Gently I picked up the harness I had crafted with such care, hating to leave it in the hands of this disgusting person. I reminded myself that I'd made it for Mr. Anderson's wedding, and Mr. Anderson had always been fair.

Things got better after that, but I was acutely aware that I was becoming more white-eyes every minute in order to survive in Grandmother Annie's world. If Scarred-by-a-Woman could see me now, how he would laugh at me!

CHAPTER 20

A MONTH AFTER RUTH LEFT, I walked in from the barn one night and found Grandmother Annie cutting up apples for a pie. There was a letter from her daughter nearby on the table. It was not the first one she had sent, but it was the first one we had discussed.

"Daniel, I don't know what to do about Ruth." She sighed impatiently. "She keeps nagging me."

I did not ask what she meant. "She wants to see you safe and happy."

"She doesn't want to feel guilty if something happens to her mother. Why can't she understand that my feet are like roots, and they have grown deep into this soil? She thinks I do not want to live here without Orville. It is because he is gone that I cannot bear to leave!"

I studied her silently. Then I said, "I understand. I love my own homeland in this way. I will stay as long you want me to. But when the time comes that you would be better off with your daughter, do not worry about me. I will leave."

Her eyes grew sad. "Did she talk to you?"

I nodded.

Grandmother Annie shook her head. "I'm sorry, Daniel. I think she might be a little . . . jealous."

"Jealous of *me?*" It was incredible.

"Yes. She loved her brothers very much, and they're both gone and now you're here. I think maybe she finds that unfair."

I could not count all the people I had lost, all but her husband at the white-eyes' hands. But I loved Grandmother Annie too much to mention them.

"I must also tell you that I've heard from the school."

"In town?" I asked, wondering whom I had now displeased.

She shook her head. "No. Carlisle."

I felt a pressure in my chest. I loved this old woman, and she loved me. We had become family. Why couldn't the white-eyes leave us alone?

"Captain Pratt does not want me to stay either?"

"He didn't say that in his letter. He just . . . offered his condolences and asked about my plans."

I waited. When she went back to her baking, I finally asked, "What did you tell him?"

"Well, I didn't tell him anything. I only got the letter last week."

"Last week? And you did not tell me until now?"

She shrugged and kept pressing out the

pie dough with her rolling pin. "It didn't seem important."

I stood for a moment, not sure what to do.

Then Grandmother Annie said, "Daniel, you're a fine young man. You've taken the business well in hand. Some day, you'll want to see the world, or marry, or take over the whole farm on your own. When that time comes, or I get so old I am a burden, we'll both know. Until then, I don't see any reason not to go on as we are. Do you?"

It was about six months later that I was awakened in the night by Grandmother Annie's scream. It was not a nightmare scream, but a scream of utter terror, the sort of scream I hadn't heard since the last attack by bluecoats on my people.

I leapt from the bed before my eyes were even open and sprinted toward the sound. Outside, I heard Roscoe barking. I do not remember thinking. I was a mass of instinct only: fear, love, duty, and an overwhelming, almost violent need to protect my own.

I found Grandmother Annie in the kitchen, her next scream cut off in mid-breath. In the darkness I could see little, but I could hear the scuffle of feet and the wrench of heavy breathing, and I knew she was not alone. I sensed as much as saw the big man who towered over her, one hand pinning her back against him, the other stifling her mouth.

In that instant, the years away from my people vanished, and I moved with the lightning speed and fearlessness of a trained Apache warrior. I struck before the intruder even knew I was there, grabbing his neck as he turned, shocked and startled, by my full-throated warcry.

Then I wrenched his neck, exactly as Uncle Angry had taught me, and he tumbled lifelessly to the hard wooden floor.

For a long, breathless moment I did not speak, and neither did Grandmother Annie. I knelt to check the attacker, to be sure he was dead, then instinctively stepped away from the body. I wanted no chance of trouble with a white-eyes ghost.

"Grandmother, are you all right?" I asked her in Apache, the words spilling out before I realized that, after all this time, I had instinctively acted as a warrior, instinctively spoken the warrior's tongue.

When she did not answer, I quickly lit the lantern, which gave an eerie cast on the kitchen and the dead man on the floor.

I repeated my question, this time in English, but Grandmother Annie still did not answer. Her mouth hung slack, and there was no color to her face. I rushed toward her, sick with dread.

To my astonishment, she stepped back, terror flooding her eyes as she pressed herself back against the wall.

"Grandmother, he is dead. He cannot hurt

you," I assured her, remembering to speak English now. "Do you need a doctor? Are you injured?"

She shook her head in a wild, panicky sort of way, and I realized that she was in shock. I laid my hand on her shoulder, to lend her my strength. Instantly she flinched away.

At last, I knew.

She was no longer frightened of the dead man. *I was the one who brought her terror.* I had lived with her so long, played the white-eyes game so well, that maybe she had forgotten who I was inside, what I had been trained to be. Maybe, sometimes, I had forgotten, too.

I was not sorry I had killed the man who might well have murdered Grandmother Annie, and I was even a bit proud that I had done it so well, so efficiently, exactly as an Apache man should do. I had protected my own and been as brave as any warrior. Any Apache woman would have been proud of me, and grateful.

But Grandmother Annie was not proud of me, or grateful, or even relieved that I had saved her from a savage white-eyes. Her whole body was trembling.

For a moment I said nothing. I did not move. Grandmother Annie did not want me to touch her! She did not even want me there. But I could not leave her alone with a dead man in her kitchen. My ears burned hot with shame and frustration. I did not know what to do.

Then I realized that Roscoe was still barking.

When I opened the kitchen door, he raced toward Grandmother Annie. She bent down and crushed him to her chest the way I had expected she would cling to me. She almost seemed to be using the dog as a shield—something big and solid to keep her safe from the killer Apache.

A rush of pain and anger clogged my throat. I felt a renewed sense of urgency, the kind I had known on the raid. Reluctantly I knelt to examine the burglar. He was white. His gun was loaded. His pockets were stuffed with money, and Grandmother Annie's savings jar lay broken near his feet. There was no question that he'd come to rob her. Surely she had heard him and tried to stop him. Most likely he was about to kill her when I had charged into the room.

None of this, I knew, would make the slightest bit of difference to the Downingville sheriff, and I knew that Grandmother Annie was too terrified to help me. The dead man was white, and I was an Indian. An Apache. A prisoner of war who had ridden with Geronimo.

"Grandmother," I insisted, "I did not mean to frighten you. I had to act quickly, to protect you from harm. I am the same Daniel that you have always known."

Annie wept as she pulled Roscoe tighter. She would not look at me.

"I will go get help," I promised bitterly.

CHAPTER TWENTY

I kept my vow to Annie. I dragged the body to the barn, where I leaped bareback on the bay and rode as fast as I could to Polly's house. I banged on the door and told her father that Annie had been attacked by a burglar. She needed a man to protect her, and a woman to hold her close. He hollered to his wife to get out of bed and join him, then bolted out of the house to hitch up his carriage. Polly ran out a moment later and I helped her swing up behind me.

"I'll go with Daniel," she called to her father. "Annie shouldn't have to wait until you get Mother there in the carriage."

She was right, of course, but I had never ridden double with a female. An Apache girl would not have leaped up behind a boy unless it was an emergency, and I guess it was.

"Why did you leave her alone?" Polly yelled in my ear as we galloped home. "What if the burglar is still around?"

There was no point in hiding the truth from her. "He can't hurt her anymore."

There was a moment's silence behind me while Polly figured out my words. She had both arms around my middle, and I felt them loosen just a little at the news.

She said nothing else until we reached the house. I helped Polly off the bay but did not dismount. She took a step toward the porch, then stopped, turned around and faced me.

"Daniel? Aren't you coming in?"

I did not lie to her. "I tried to comfort her, but she was afraid of me."

Polly took a step back in my direction. "Daniel, I'm sure she realized that you saved her life."

"No," I answered darkly, "she only knows I killed someone."

Before Polly could reply, Annie's shaky voice called out from the house. "Polly, are thee out there?"

Polly hollered back, glanced at me, and rushed inside. A moment later I heard Annie sobbing. Her voice rose higher than I had ever heard it. She was almost hysterical.

"Daniel killed him," she was sobbing brokenly. "He just leaped in the air with a terrible warwhoop, then twisted that man's neck and snapped it! He looked just like a murdering Apache on the warpath! I'd almost forgotten he was an Indian."

So had I. Oh, not completely, not forever, but some part of me, born of desperation, had come to believe that I had a life as a harness maker, a life with the Hamiltons.

Nobody needed to tell me I'd been wrong.

CHAPTER 21

I TOOK NOTHING that did not belong to me. I ran to my cache, which I had never revealed to anyone. I had not looked inside the circle of rocks in over a year—since the day the Hamiltons had made me kin—but I knew that everything a warrior must have was hidden there.

Never let the white-eyes find you, my uncle's voice came to me. *Hide first. Run later. You can catch or kill whatever you need.*

The Quakers, I knew, would surround Annie while she was in shock. It might be days before they even noticed I was missing. I felt bad about the many chores I had left undone, but the men would fill in. Some would say, "I'm not surprised. What can thee expect from an Indian?"

It was fall. The leaves were thick on the ground, and noisy. I had no moccasins, only hard-heeled boots. I was wearing a cowhide coat, but I had no hat or rain gear. No horse, no fresh food. And—I realized this all too soon—absolutely nowhere to go.

I tried to think like my enemy. The sheriff would come after me. He would think like a white man, expecting me to hide in the fields nearby, or rush back to Carlisle, or run to my people in prison. Even if I could face my uncle, I could not risk his safety.

This meant I must go some other way, somewhere no one would look for me and somewhere I could not be found. East meant more cities, and they would look for me south and west. I would run north, straight to the Appalachian Mountains Miss Lawson had shown me in her book of maps. Even if the white-eyes searched such rugged country, they could never find an Apache who did not want to be found.

I ran all night, trying to find the slow, steady pace that Uncle Angry had taught me. He had also taught me to hide during the day, but I knew this was a risk I could not take. So close to Downingville, the land was too flat and filled with people for me to find any fool-proof hiding place. I must be as careful as possible and press on.

I kept off the backroads and ran through the harvested, unplanted fields of autumn. This time of year there was little reason for the farmers to be tending them. Once I saw a black man, at a distance, and I ducked away. Another time I had to cross a road and saw a freckle-faced boy carrying a fishing pole. I could not hide from him, so I forced myself to smile and wave. I did nothing that would cause him to remember me.

I had been trained to go for days without

sleeping, but my Child-of-the-Water days seemed quite distant to me now. I knew I could make better time at night, and I surely would not last if I did not get some rest. I finally found a deserted cornfield and hid my rawhide carrying pouch among the rows. Then I dug a shallow ditch, stretched out in it, and covered myself with dead cornstalks and dried out cobs.

Despite my terrible fatigue, I was too tense to fall asleep, and I only dozed. By nightfall it began to rain. I was tempted to dump my wet, bulky blanket, but I knew it would save my life in the mountains when winter came.

Again I ran all night and into the morning. At daybreak I found myself in such open fields that someone could have spotted me, or heard my low cough. The only place I found to hide was a burned-out barn that was heavily overgrown with sticker-weeds and ivy. I could not imagine that anyone would come here except for children seeking a secret place to play. I checked carefully, but I found no sign of humans in recent days.

I collapsed in deep sleep for hours. By the time I woke up it was full dark. I was ravenous. I had not eaten for two nights and a whole day. My white-eyes canteen was nearly empty, and the water inside was tinny-tasting. I decided to go hunting tonight and risk one more day in the burned-out barn.

I had only my spear, my knife, and a rawhide slingshot. I crept out into the night like a hunter—or a hunted thing—and searched for the glowing eyes of an opossum, or even a mole. I have no idea how long I stumbled around in the darkness, too exhausted to remember all I had been taught, too unsure of the land and too afraid of discovery to hunt effectively. Once, when I thought I was going to catch an opossum, I began to cough and startled the creature. By the time I threw my rock, it had waddled off.

It was almost morning before I found a large squirrel. This time, when I drew my slingshot, my aim was true. I captured the squirrel while it lay there, stunned, and smashed its head beneath my foot. In desperation, I ate it on the spot. I dared not risk building a fire, so there was no point in waiting until I returned to my temporary shelter.

I thought of Annie, and the great pride she took in her cooking. How I loved her food! What would she think of me, squatting like a wolf over my fresh-killed prey, my jaws dripping with blood? I felt like an animal.

I shook my head, and saw my uncle's face. Had I really begun to think like a white-eyes? I had done nothing wrong. I had defended someone I loved, struck to kill, and used my skills to escape and survive! I was not a white-eyes child who had failed to become a harness maker.

I was a boy who had been trained since birth to become an Apache brave.

It took me five days to reach the mountains, and it rained almost continuously. By the time

CHAPTER TWENTY-ONE

I was certain that no white-eyes sheriff had followed me—or could find me if he had—I was far above farming land, surrounded by bushes, protected by lofty orange-and-gold leaved trees.

I was also coughing so steadily that I could not have hidden from any man. I was exhausted from the long run and lack of food. I had eaten nothing but the squirrel, one mole, and two gamebirds since the night I ran away. I was so hungry I could have eaten an elk.

It was colder in the mountains, even when it did not rain. I knew it was finally safe to build a fire, to set up a tiny home. Of course I found no abandoned barn in the wilderness, or even a dilapidated miner's shack. I knew I had no choice. I must build a wickiup.

This was a job I had never done, nor ever been trained to do. It was women's work, and Apache girls were very good at it. I did the best I could.

First I found a sheltered spot where it would be hard for the blustery wind or white-eyes to find me. There were no junipers or mesquites in these mountains, so I had to settle for a cluster of small birch saplings. I cut them off with my knife. Without even digging a trench, I forced them into the ground and tied their tops together with some long weeds. Then I covered them with all the brush I could find and laid the dirty blanket over the top.

The wickiup was half the size of the ones I had grown up with, just big enough for the fire and me. I couldn't figure out how Apache women released the smoke through the roof, so I put the fire by the door to let the smoke escape and to keep the wild creatures out. I did not know these mountains, but I suspected that they might well shelter bears and poisonous snakes and wolves.

There might be deer here, too, and it was venison I craved above all else. If I could kill a buck, I could eat my fill, dry the rest, and still have food for days. And I would need it—lots of it—if the sickness had its way.

As I lay by the fire, rolling over from time to time to heat another chilly part of me, I considered all my options. They were no better than they had been before. I could not risk capture.

Slowly it came to me that aside from the wilderness, the best place to hide a Chiricahua would be in a group of Apaches. And White Mountain Apaches, if not Chiricahuas, still filled the land I loved above all others.

Home.

I slept most of the day after I made my wickiup, lulled by the joyful warmth of my own fire. I felt very weak, coughed a lot and often had to fight for breath. But hunger gnawed at me incessantly, and I knew I had to stir myself and find some meat.

Early in the morning of the second day, I took my spear and hunted for what seemed like hours, but wearing my heavy riding boots, I never seemed to be able to sneak up on game.

When night fell, I finally spotted an opossum, which did not even try to get away. I cooked it—a joy to be sure—and slept another day.

Every morning, my cough was worse. Still I kept on hunting. By now I realized that I needed a better way to bring down food. I would not grow strong on rodents and season-thin songbirds. I started working on a bow and arrows. This was not easy, partly because I had no time to cure the wood and no way to break a branch from a mulberry tree. I had to make do with green oak. At first I could not recall everything my uncle and One-Who-Remembers had taught me, but as I worked with the wood, it slowly came back to me. Still, it took me over a week to create usable weapons.

Once the bow was ready, hunting was much easier. I had spent years with a bow and arrow in my hands, and my fingers and eyes knew exactly what to do. My first few arrows were not very straight and frightened off game without hitting any. But I worked again, hunger driving me on, until I had a fine straight arrow with three smooth feathers.

The next morning, just after dawn, I brought down a four-point buck. I said the proper warrior's prayers. For the first time in ten days, a smile slipped across my weary face.

I could feel my uncle's pride.

I did not try to move my camp until I had regained my health and had dried enough food to travel. I fashioned a buckskin carrying-bag to haul with a tumpline around my shoulders, Apache-man style. My strength—and my pride—were slowly returning. I had faced disaster and survived. It wasn't the same as a fourth Child-of-the-Water raid, but it proved there was still enough Apache in me to someday become a warrior.

I do not know how many weeks went by as I eased my way southwestward through the mountains. As the trees grew bare and snow began to fall, I never escaped the penetrating cold. I moved fast by day and huddled at night by the fire. Sometimes I spotted poor folks' shacks, but I always found a way to go around them. I could not afford to be seen until I came to a place where I could be mistaken for a local Indian.

Bit by bit, I replaced my white-eyes clothes with the skin of whatever I killed. I made knee-high moccasins and a buckskin shirt—simple, no fringe, but it kept me warm and made me feel like an Apache. My thick black hair began to grow out again until it almost touched my shoulders.

By the time I came to the base of the Appalachians and crossed into Arkansas several months later, I felt proud once more to be Solito. If "Daniel Hamilton" still lived, he was buried deep inside me, and I didn't care if I ever saw him again.

CHAPTER 22

I DID NOT REACH CHIRICAHUA country until early spring. In my mind it was the Moon-When-the-Leaf-Buds-Are-Swelling, but I knew that Annie would call it April, or maybe late March. I had not kept track of the days in white-eyes style. I knew only that I was nearly home.

The changes were hard to pinpoint at first. The aspen leaves were only tiny humps of green, and the snow was dirty slush. But the sun seemed to rise a little earlier and I had more time to hunt before it set. The nights were not as terribly cold and sometimes I could even go without a fire.

I had lived through this season twice in Pennsylvania, but nothing there was like spring in Arizona. The eastern white-eyes had always asked me how I could love a land of sand and rock and cactus. It had no color, no life, no joy, they'd said to me. Fools! In the spring, Mother Earth painted herself with a thousand shades of bloom—purple owl-clover, white ajo-lilies, yellow-eyed prickly poppies! The ironwood sprouted beautiful lavender flowers. Here and there a cactus wore little hats of pink and red! Oh, yes, there were signs of spring on the Hamiltons' farm, but not one bud or blossom could make it shine like the land of my birth.

There were other changes, too. At night, though I was still alone, I could hear the sounds of my brother-animals nearby in the hills. Sometimes I could hear coyotes howl or a puma scream. I saw signs of grizzlies—twice the size of the bears that roamed the Appalachians. The farther west I walked, the fewer people I had to dodge. And in the last month or so, I'd started to smell boiling beans and half-cooked venison when I passed a ranch, and even roasted rattler once. The rich aroma of pine grew more potent, more glorious, with each passing day.

Then one sunny morning, as the mist and fog cleared while I put out my morning fire, I spotted snow-capped mountains to the west. Not the scrawny red-clay hills of Arkansas where I had passed the winter, but the brilliant, sparkling, sky-piercing White Mountains that my birth family surely still called home.

Four days later, I found my way to a cache I had visited once when we were on the run with Geronimo. Like all Chiricahua hideaways, it was so well hidden that no one who did not know where it was would ever spot it.

For several minutes, I stared at the huge lodgepole pine that marked the tiny cave, taking in the sight and smell of this first moment of my homecoming. I remembered watching my aunt carefully pad and assemble the inside of this rocky crevice! On the surface, I saw no sign of my people now, but I knew I had been here with them, on the edge of Chiricahua territory. If my uncle had been with me, he would have sighed with quiet pleasure.

I did the same. I had achieved no small victory! I had escaped a conviction for a white-eyes killing I could not avoid. I had dodged human beings for five full months. I had taken care of myself in the wilderness as only an Apache can.

And yet, there was a part of me that still did not feel like a man. I certainly looked like one. My muscles had grown solid, almost hard. I was half a foot taller than I had been the last time I had stood beneath this tree. My brain had sharpened and my heart had grown tough.

But in my soul I knew I had never finished my time as Child-of-the-Water, which meant I was not yet a true warrior. How could I feel like a man when I had never proven myself in battle? And how could I ever undertake another raid? My time in Pennsylvania had ruined me for a lifetime of stealing from white-eyes. I had discovered that some of them did have souls. I had learned to love their books, enjoy their sports, and even relish some of their cooking. I actually missed Polly, Roscoe, and the bay.

Bitterly I fought memories of Annie. I still remembered how she and He-Who-Was-My-Grandfather had hugged me the morning after I had learned that She-Who-Was-My-Mother had died. *That* had been a moment of homecoming, a moment of family. My arrival in Chiricahua country should have been the same, but this triumph rang hollow in my heart. I had finally made my way home, but no one waited for me here.

No one waited for me anywhere.

I bundled up my feelings as I approached the cache, not certain what I would find here after all these years. In a way, it did not matter: I was not being chased, nor was I particularly low on supplies. But I needed proof, somehow, that this was still my country, still the land where Apaches lived in total harmony with Yusn.

I walked to the tree and lay down my bow and quiver, careful to keep my knife at my side. I had stood for long enough to note any sound of trouble, but that did not keep me from being careful. Slowly I edged to the side of the tree and started to pull off the layers of pebbles and dried grass.

I was looking for piñon nuts or dried beef wrapped in buckskin. There should have been a pitched woven water *tus*. A back-up knife. Maybe even a blanket.

At first I found nothing. This land was smothered with lodgepole pines, and I wondered if my memory had failed me. Was it too late for me to come back to my own country? Had I imagined peace here after all this time?

And then I struck it . . . a pitched *tus* that all but shredded when my knife pierced its side.

My heart thumped at the familiar sight. It was empty and falling apart, but it had once been placed here by my tribe.

But my people were gone, and so were the supplies I had hoped to find. No animal had clawed the cache. It had been opened and used. Whoever took the food had not bothered to replace it. This was not the Apache way.

The abandoned cache saddened me more than I wanted to admit. I had planned to camp in this secluded, familiar spot, but now I could not bear it. Before I left, I reburied the broken *tus* and stroked the rough bark of lodgepole pine.

The next day I came across a small white-eyes town that had sprung up while I had been away. I had not expected it and barely managed to dodge a pair of curly-haired boys racing their ponies down a sorry mountain trail. On the edge of the dusty main street, a freshly painted sign proclaimed: "Welcome to Riley's Ridge. Biggest Little Town in the Mountains."

I dropped and melted into the scrub, wondering what the locals would think if they spotted me. We were so close to the boundaries of the Fort Apache Reservation that surely Apaches were a common sight. And yet, I wasn't sure I could hide myself here. I didn't *feel* like a reservation Apache, or think like one, and I feared I would say or do something to reveal my Carlisle training. Such an error could be fatal if the Pennsylvania authorities had notified the reservation agent or the troop commander at Fort Apache that a "murderer" from Carlisle might be making his way back home. I could even draw attention by acting educated.

When the boys were gone, I carefully skirted the town, my nose picking up the sweet smell of new sawdust and the acrid one of freshly tanned leather. I found myself wondering if Riley's Ridge had a harness maker, let alone someone skilled enough to craft saddles. Instinctively my fingers curved around an imaginary bent-awl, and I fought back the hungry memory of the fine leather work in which I'd taken such pride.

If I were white, I could stop right here and start a business, I thought abruptly. *If I had not killed a man.* It startled me how much the thought appealed to me: establishing my white-eyes trade in the very mountains of my Apache homeland.

I pushed the futile dream from my mind and pressed on. I soon came upon the great rushing river close to where She-Who-Was-My-Mother had first found me. I had seen it before, when we'd briefly lived on the reservation, and it was just as full this spring as it had been then. I remembered my uncle warning me about flash floods this time of year . . . when the winter-packed snow finally melts and races madly down the mountains.

I kept the possibility in the back of my mind as I moved downriver for several miles. It was raining hard, but I did not stop because I had a good overnight place in mind. Geronimo's band had kept a good cache in a cave just south of here. It was more protected than any other camping spot within miles, and it was roomy enough inside for a blazing fire.

I briefly stopped to eat a piece of venison jerky, then pressed on, certain that I would reach the cave by nightfall. And I would have, too, if the snowpack I had passed that morning had not abruptly wrenched loose from its peak.

I do not know when it happened, or where it started. I only know that suddenly I could hear the river boiling crazily even though I was now two or three miles beyond it. There was a chance, a very good chance, that the water would spill its banks, and if that happened, I wanted to be too high up the side of the cliff for it to catch me.

I started to run—not the slow, easy run that an Apache can keep up for miles, but the desperate sprinting he does when he's dodging the bullets of his enemies. For a few minutes, I thought I might make it to safety.

Then I heard the roar of the water splashing ferociously toward me, and when I turned around, I could see that the river had leaped its banks.

Running would not save me. Not even an Apache could outrun a flash flood! I was fairly close to the cave but not close enough—not when I hadn't been there in nearly three years and would need a little time to find it. The water might be coming too fast for me to even reach the rocks at the base of the cliff.

In the few seconds it took me to consider the best plan, the water charged closer, so close I could almost feel its spray. I wasted no more time on thinking. I did the only thing I could. I ran to the trunk of the nearest tree.

It was not the tallest one, or the strongest one, or even the one with the sturdiest branches. It was *there,* that was all, and I scrambled up to the top while I prayed for Yusn to save me.

Then I heard a scream, a terrible scream, a scream cut off by the sound of the madly-churning water. I looked down and saw a crush of light-colored hair flopping wildly about a hundred yards from my perch. A swirl of wet fabric, big enough for a white-eyes skirt, billowed under an air pocket in the water. One lacy-drawer-clad leg looked tangled in the sodden cloth.

I am not sure what happened next. I only know that I was swept out of the branches as the force of the water repeatedly slammed against me. Once it smashed me down on the rocky river bed, and when I came up I saw no safe place to land.

I could still hear the girl screaming.

I forgot her as I battled the vicious current, fighting it tooth and nail as I bobbed up and down. The muddy froth rushed over me, filling my nose and mouth until I could not breathe. Still I pressed on, determined to stay afloat until I reached solid ground.

And then, abruptly, I found myself flung against a granite boulder. At first I could not crawl up on its slippery surface. All I did was let it hold me steady, blocking the force of the current that sought to drag me under. Several times I lunged to the top but the water always knocked me back down. By the time I finally clawed my way to the top of the boulder, the girl was screaming once again.

I spotted her downstream, swimming madly, as I had, toward the southern bank of the thrashing river. She was stronger than I expected, but greatly hampered by her heavy skirt. Repeatedly the water flipped her over, pounding her with waves and debris.

She was almost beyond my line of vision when the river dashed her onto a patch of mud, then thundered across her still body.

"Are you all right?" I hollered above the roar.

But of course she did not answer. Even if she could hear me, she surely had no strength to yell.

Once more the water washed over her, and still she did not rise. I could not tell if she was breathing. I only knew that the frothing waves would soon smother her if she didn't move to higher ground.

"Crawl up to that line of trees!" I hollered.

She did not move.

"The river's still rising! Go now!"

The current plowed over her again and flipped her onto her back. That's when I knew she'd used up every last drop of her strength and had surely passed out.

Or was already dead.

CHAPTER 23

I HAD PROMISED MYSELF, since the day I left Annie's, that I would have nothing to do with white-eyes ever again. I had vowed that until I was safe on Apache land, I would make contact with no living person. Anyone could betray me. But I had tried to help this girl instinctively when we'd both faced desperation. Now she faced certain death if I would not—could not—rescue her. If she were Polly, I knew I could not turn away.

She was not Polly, and I did not know her. But I remembered only too well Annie's lessons: *You should think of anyone in need as your family. Every girl is Polly. Orville is every man.*

I pushed away common sense and dove off the rock, letting the river push me downstream. We fought hard, the river and I, but in the end I won. I was beached a good thirty yards past the girl, but I could still see her brightly colored clothing flopping in the water.

I ran to the white girl's side. Her face was dark with mud and her hair was a maze of knots and twigs. One long sleeve had been torn off her dress. She wore no shoes. She still did not move.

"Can you breathe?" I asked when I reached her, afraid I had arrived too late. Roughly I dragged her up toward the trees, safe from the river's pull for the moment. I rolled her on her side and slapped her back. Water spewed out of her mouth, and then she coughed.

Thank you, Yusn, I whispered.

"Can you get up?" I called above the roar of the river.

She opened her eyes and took a deep breath. There was terror in those big, hazel eyes, but I couldn't tell whether it was the water or me that she feared so greatly. In the roiling river, it would have been hard for her to identify me as an Apache. Up close, there couldn't have been much doubt.

"We've got to move!" I yelled at her. "The river is still rising!"

She took another deep breath and rolled to her knees. She tried to stand up, but sagged against me, trembling.

"Can you walk?" I asked.

She nodded yes. She tried. After three slow paces she fell to her knees. She lost consciousness again.

I looked back at the river. I tried to remember what I'd been taught about white girls, and how to treat them, and how *not* to treat them to stay out of trouble.

Then I remembered what I knew about staying alive.

I slung her across my shoulders as though she were a fresh-killed deer. A white man, I knew, would never touch a decent woman's ankles; an Apache would not touch a decent woman's heels. So I gripped her wrists in my left hand and reluctantly clutched the back of one knee with the right.

Then I started running. Slow, steady, the way I had been trained, with a power that the white-eyes boys in Pennsylvania had never known. Uncle Angry had taught me that a warrior can ignore pain, ignore fatigue, ignore hunger, and even thirst, for days if he has to, to save himself or those he loves. I did not know this white girl, and, as weak as I was after my battle with the river, the burden of carrying her was almost overwhelming. But Annie's voice ran with me, right along with Uncle Angry's, and I knew I could not face my grandmother's memory if I tossed the white girl down.

We did not make it to the cave by dark. In my confused fatigue, I searched for it several times in places it was not, and I was staggering under my load by the time I spotted the crest of rocks that signaled I had finally reached my goal.

The girl had moved little during the last long hour, and she did not stir now. I wanted nothing more than to drop her to the earth and gather wood to start a fire. But just as I spotted the cave's stony face, I was startled by the sound of a horse galloping toward us at full thundering speed. The hoofbeats were almost smothered by a piercing Apache warcry.

I had not heard such a terrifying sound from

another man for years, but I reacted without a moment's fatal hesitation. Instinctively I dropped the girl behind a rocky outgrowth and reached for my bow, forgetting that I had lost it in the river. I grabbed for my knife as the horse bore down on me and the still-shrieking rider flung himself to the ground. He hit me hard, hard enough to drop my knife and send me rolling. The horse skittered off a yard or two as the other man struggled to grab my hair with one hand. He stabbed me in the shoulder with the other.

The blade ripped my flesh wide open, but I did not make a sound. I slammed my forearms against the Apache's wrists, then reached desperately for his knife. In that instant, as he threw his head back and yelled again, Moon flashed across his face. In sudden confusion, I sensed that something was all wrong with this fight. He was not the enemy. Neither was I.

I spotted four long scars on his cheek.

Without thinking I screamed, "Scarred-by-a-Woman! Do you not know your own kin?"

He froze for just a second, long enough for me to break his grip. His knife clattered between us as I yelled again, "We rode together with Geronimo! Have you forgotten that my cousin was your brother's wife?"

This time he stopped cold and stared at me. I knew he could kill me in an instant. In my current condition I was not strong enough to beat him one-on-one. My only safety lay in taking my old boyhood role, the one I hated.

"You used to call me Little-Left-Behind."

He laughed. He laughed long and hard, with a sharp, cruel edge to his laughter that I did not recall. He slapped my face with the affection of a grizzly greeting her runt cub and laughed again.

"Little-Left-Behind! You are the last of them I thought would survive."

I wasn't sure what he meant by that and I wasn't sure I wanted to. All that mattered was that he didn't seem intent on killing me anymore.

Then I remembered that I had carried a white girl to an Apache hiding place, and if he discovered her, he would kill her for sure.

"I killed a white-eyes," I told him roughly, stalling for time. "It has taken me a long time to get home."

He leaped to his feet then, his dark, hate-filled eyes testing me for a moment. "Tell me what happened to my brother."

The truth was grim. "He was killed trying to escape. His wife and baby still live in a white-eyes fort."

He turned away, his shame, for that one instant, unbearable. I don't know what would have happened next if the forest had surrounded his grief with silence. Instead, we were both surprised by the sudden thunder of a horse galloping off at a dead run.

I knew the girl had stolen his mount before Scarred-by-a-Woman did. I had saved her life and she had betrayed me! I should have expected no less from a white-eyes.

Scarred-by-a-Woman whistled sharply for the pony, but there was no response. At once he turned on me, the knife sharply raised.

"Did you sell me to the bluecoats?"

"No! I would never—"

"Coward! I knew you would never become an Apache brave!"

My shoulder burned and my heart sagged. He was right—oh, how he had always been right!—and I was too numb to prove him otherwise. I had triumphantly traveled two thousand miles alone in the dead of winter, only to be betrayed by the first white person I spoke to and nearly murdered by the first Apache.

Abruptly I realized that my legs were shaking. My arm and shoulder were drenched in blood. I no longer cared about the girl or this hate-filled brave whom I had once proudly numbered among my distant kin. I wanted nothing more than to crawl into the cave.

"I need a fire," I begged him, too desperate to feign strength. "Do you have anything clean to stop the bleeding?"

He did not answer me. He cocked his head to the west, the direction the horse had gone. I knew what he heard. I, too, could feel the pounding of hooves vibrating in the ground beneath me.

This wasn't one horse, and it wasn't going

away. It was a whole herd, or a group of riders, heading toward us at a deadly pace.

I shivered violently, knowing now that a fire would not be enough to save me. The bluecoats were coming—after me, after Scarred-by-a-Woman, after the girl?—and I was too weak to run now. I had lost so much blood! Without Scarred-by-a-Woman's help, I could not escape.

I was almost unconscious now, but my lifetime of Apache training swirled in my head. No matter what had happened, no matter what years and deaths and miseries now lay between us, Scarred-by-a-Woman and I still belonged to the same tribe. If I called his name, he could *not* fail to help me.

"Scarred-by-a-Woman!" I yelled with all my might.

He spared me only a glance before he raced away.

CHAPTER 24

AS THE HOOFBEATS POUNDED closer, I had only one choice: crawl into the dense layer of wet leaves and bury myself before the soldiers reached me. I knew this instinctively, just as I knew that I if I spent the night on the soggy earth, I would freeze to death. But surrender was not a choice. Better to fight to the end and die a wounded warrior, to spend eternity in The Happy Place.

I tried to stand, but found I was too weak to rise above my knees. I tried anyway, half-stumbling, dragging myself toward safety until a huge bluecoat seized my soaking shirt and slammed me to the ground.

Pointing a rifle at my head, he kicked me with his boot and yelled, "Hey, Sergeant! Let's make this buck talk before he dies!"

I could hear the jangle of stirrups and canteens, but all I could see were horses' hooves and white-eyes boots—the kind I had discarded somewhere in the Appalachians.

"It's not Scarred-by-a-Woman, but I'll bet he can tell us where he's gone!"

Someone with a scrawny beard leaned over

me and slugged me in the jaw. "You-um tell-um me where Injun went-um, and maybe you live-um, you understand me?"

If I had not been facing the end of my life, I would have laughed at his ridiculous attempt at "Apache" English, but I had no humor left in my soul. I only knew that I must do as my uncle had taught me. *Never tell the white-eyes what they want to know. Never betray another member of the tribe. Never forget you are an Apache.*

"You hear the sergeant, boy?" Big Bluecoat hollered again. He cocked his pistol and pointed it at my head. "You tell us where your chief has gone or you'll never see daylight again!"

Without thinking, I knocked the gun out of his hand, pulled up my knees and kicked him in the throat. I tried to rise and run away, but another soldier—or two or three—slammed me back down on the ground and battered me with rifle butts until I was numb.

I came to slowly, feeling woozy and uncertain in my body and my mind. I was shivering almost convulsively. I hurt all over. For some reason that I could not quite figure out, I felt ashamed and betrayed.

"He cannot be my son," I heard an old man say in Apache. "Tell the captain that I have seen the ghost of He-Who-Was-My-Son. Long ago he was killed by the one with the scars. If the blue-coats found this boy with the Evil One, he is an outlaw, too." His voice grew dark with sorrow. *"He cannot be my son."*

A second voice repeated the words of the first one, in English this time. I could make no sense of it.

I writhed on cold concrete, not natural ground. My throbbing shoulder pressed against iron bars, and my ribs felt broken. Blood caked my filthy, river-drenched shirt. Wherever I was, I had received no dry blankets, no clean clothes, and certainly no medical care.

"Tell him to look at the boy anyway," a third voice replied in English. "I want to know who he is."

I did not recognize the voice, but I knew it was the Voice of Power. This man was a chief, or the bluecoat version of Captain Pratt. I was too dizzy to remember where I was, but I knew it could not be Carlisle. And I knew that I'd been running from the law.

Slowly I opened my eyes and tried to focus on the men. One was white, in full uniform. One was Apache, wearing a cowboy hat, a plaid shirt, and a pair of Army trousers. The third was elderly and dressed the way my uncle did—in a long breechcloth and knee-high moccasins. He wore a loose-sleeved shirt and a red sash around his head. In every way, he looked like the old-time White Mountain Apaches I had left on the reservation.

When I stared at him, I saw absolute terror snake across his sun-leathered face. He took a step back, one hand outstretched as though to ward off an evil spirit. I had never seen the old man before, but I had the eerie feeling that he knew me.

"This Apache boy looks like your son, the one that chased after Scarred-by-a-Woman when that beast took your daughter," said the officer to the old one. "You telling me he *doesn't* look familiar?"

The whitemanized Apache translated again, but this time the frightened old man did not respond. He would not look at me.

"You know him! I can see it on your face. If he's not your boy, who is he?"

I decided that I should be the one to answer that question. In spite of all the trouble I'd had in Pennsylvania, I knew that "Daniel Hamilton" might be able to play the white-eyes game well enough to keep from hanging. "Solito" didn't have a chance if the Army thought he rode with a killer renegade.

Somehow I found my voice. "I can tell you my name, sir," I said with all the Carlisle decorum I could muster. I was ashamed at how easily the whitemanized words rolled off my tongue, how quickly I put survival over pride.

An eerie silence fell among the men. The captain squinted his eyes and poked his head right up to the bars to see me better.

"Well, who are you? And how come you don't speak English like the local Indians? Aren't you an Apache?"

I struggled to sit up, cross-legged, knowing I should have stood but lacking the strength to do so. "I was educated at Carlisle Indian School. They named me Daniel Hamilton."

The two Apaches looked stunned by my little speech. The frightened one touched the interpreter's sleeve, silently asking for a translation. They exchanged a few words, too soft for me to hear.

The officer said, "That explains why you talk like that, but it doesn't explain what you're doing here. Or how long you've been riding with Scarred-by-a-Woman."

I didn't want to talk about Scarred-by-a-Woman, at least not until I had more information. It was one thing for a Chiricahua to make war on the white-eyes and Mexicans, another altogether to randomly kill White Mountain Apaches.

"I knew him several years ago," I confessed uneasily, "but I ran into him at the cave by accident. I had just crawled out of the flood. Maybe he had, too."

"Ha!" the captain jeered. "You brought him a white girl! Are you going to tell me that was a coincidence, too?"

My tongue felt thick. I had not spoken this much in a very long time. "The girl was trapped in the river. I did what I could for her."

This time the captain laughed out loud. "I'll wire Carlisle to confirm your name, but nobody's going to buy the rest of your tale. I hope my lieutenant can persuade you to tell us more about your outlaw-friend."

Abruptly, the old-time Apache said to me, "Were you with him when he killed my boy and stole my girl?"

Without waiting for directions, the interpreter said, "Scarred-by-a-Woman took the old one's daughter two years ago. Her brother, the one who looks like you, vowed to bring her back at any cost. Somehow he helped her escape, but she came home alone. We never found his body, but since then the old man has seen the ghost of his son."

"What did you say?" the white chief demanded.

The interpreter pretended he had not heard.

Stirred to anger, I vowed to the old one, "I was raised a Chiricahua, but I have not seen Scarred-by-a-Woman since Geronimo's band was sent away. And even if I had, I would *never* harm another Apache.

"I came back to join the White Mountain Apaches because this is Yusn's land and all my Chiricahua people went to prison. Now they are dead or dying. I was born in the White Mountains and I hoped I might find someone left from my birth family here."

I paused to gather enough strength to keep talking. "I told the truth to the white-eyes. I know nothing about your children, and I was only trying to help the white girl."

Suddenly the cell block grew silent again. The old man was staring at me in a strange new way. He looked sad and troubled and confused.

At last he said to the interpreter, "Tell the

captain that if he does not clean this boy's wound and get him dry, he will not live long enough to put him on the Evil One's trail."

I didn't know whether to feel grateful or misused.

A narrow-eyed lieutenant showed up outside my cell two hours later. Two burly privates stood guard as he barged in with a revolver and demanded roughly that I tell him everything I knew about Scarred-by-a-Woman's habits and future plans. It might mean the difference between a jail sentence, he threatened me, or being hung.

"I have been gone too long to know where he will go to ground," I said truthfully, but I did not add that three years ago, I had shared his horse while he had slipped in and out of dozens of his best-hidden secret places in the Chiricahua Mountains. "Even if I could remember all our strongholds, I could not give you directions. These are things I learned as an Apache boy, and I would have to track Scarred-by-a-Woman myself to remember all of them."

"I suppose that if we were foolish enough to let you go, you would bring him back for us?" The lieutenant sneered.

My shoulders straightened. "I would never track down another Apache for you!" *Maybe for that troubled old man,* I added to myself, *if his dreadful tale is true. But I would only turn Scarred-by-a-Woman over to our own people for Apache justice. I could never betray a Chiricahua to a white-eyes.*

The lieutenant did not take no for an answer. He pressed me some more, but I would reveal nothing about our hideaways.

"Tell me about Pennsylvania," the lieutenant demanded. "Why did you leave? And why did you come back here?"

"Where else would I go?" I asked straightforwardly. "I was born in this land. It is my home."

He glared at me but did not answer. "You didn't say why you left Carlisle."

"I was part of the outing system. I was placed on a farm."

"And what did you do on this farm?"

I became a member of the family. I almost forgot I was an Apache. I killed a man.

Outloud I said, "I was trained as a harness maker. The man who taught me was very good."

"So why did you run away from him?"

My skin grew tight. "I would never have left him! He is . . . of this world no longer."

"And they sent you back to Carlisle when he died?"

I was running out of honest answers, and I did not want to tell him about the burglar. But what else was there to say?

"You know we'll find out when we wire Carlisle," the lieutenant threatened, "so you might as well tell me the truth right now."

I shivered again. My body throbbed all over.

Suddenly I knew that no matter what I did or said, I was going to be killed anyway. There was no way out of this canyon.

"A white man robbed the harness maker's widow and tried to harm her," I told the lieutenant honestly. "I stopped him. She was safe."

The officer cocked his head to one side. "You mean you murdered a white man?"

I shook my head. "Murder is when you have no good reason to take another man's life. I merely killed him."

"You're saying you had no other choice?" he asked in disbelief.

I thought of Annie, and how much we had both loved He-Who-Was-My-Grandfather. Suddenly I could feel no more bitterness toward her, only the great tenderness in which she had always wrapped me. The forgiveness was sweet and cleansing, even in this darkest hour of my life.

"She is family," I said simply. "I had no choice."

CHAPTER 25

AFTER THE LIEUTENANT LEFT, I saw no one else that day but the guard who shoved one dry blanket, a bowl of soft porridge, and some biscuits between the bars to me. He gave me no utensils, and, when I asked for a spoon, he laughed. As the days passed in the stinking cage, I lost more strength, and my hope all but died. At last I fully understood why my people had stopped fighting the white-eyes, why Geronimo had finally come in, why White-Man's-Dog had found life easier licking the white-eyes' boots than standing tall. There was no way to win. I would always be an Indian, a savage, to these people, who did not know that they were the savages themselves.

This, I realized, was the worst thing they had done to us. It wasn't the killing, the rape of the land, or the destruction of our culture. It was what they left us when they took our land and freedom: nothing but despair.

I had been in the darkened guardhouse for two or three days when I heard a white girl talking to a guard outside. For an instant I thought of Polly, but I knew she was not here.

I did not recognize the young voice, nor that of an older man who spoke as well. I was not paying much attention until two guards arrived, carrying chains, and glared at me through the bars.

"Some folks here to see you," the taller one said. "Don't ask me why. This hole is no place for a lady, so you gotta come outside. Gonna put chains on you first and watch your every move, so don't try nothing, boy. Captain says to shoot you at the first sign of trouble."

I said nothing as he opened the cell. I did not want to see anyone. I was too ashamed. I was still in pain and badly bruised. Two of my ribs were broken. My stiff shoulder wound throbbed. I had been denied any chance to bathe or wear clean clothes, and even the dry blanket I had been given trembled with lice.

The chains were heavy on my wrists, worse yet on my ankles. I did not feel human as the guard prodded me from the cell. I could not remember the last time I had been a child.

"Papa, this is the Indian I was telling you about," the white girl chirped when she saw me.

Sheepishly I glanced at her. She was a pretty girl, blond with lively hazel eyes and a mouth that smiled instinctively. I felt too miserable to smile back.

The older man studied me. "I, uh, understand I owe you a great debt, boy. Lizzie tells me you saved her life."

That woke me up a little. I turned back to the girl and tried to imagine her soaked and battered by the flood. Truthfully, I had never really noticed her face. I had rescued her for Annie and Polly, not for herself.

From the moment of my capture, I'd been sorry I had.

"Do you understand me, boy?" the man said loudly.

Resentfully I glared in his direction. "My English is more than adequate, sir, and my hearing is just fine."

He blushed, but Lizzie giggled.

"I told you he spoke great English, Papa. He kept asking if I was all right."

I turned back to the girl. It was hard to stay mad at someone with such a sunny disposition. Besides, she had come to thank me. Most white girls would never have ventured anywhere near an injured Indian in a jail cell.

"I am glad that you are well. I did not mean to drop you on the ground so hard. There was no time to be gentle."

She grinned at me. "I know. When I saw the scars on the other Indian's face, I knew who he had to be, so I figured you were going to die. He's killed so many people!" She fiddled with a tiny purse in her hands. "Please forgive me for just leaving you there. I guess I was only thinking of myself." She looked away, true regret darkening her kind eyes. "I was so certain he would kill you and then . . . hurt me. All I could think of was getting away."

"*I* had a chance with him," I declared with a hint of Chiricahua pride.

Lizzie's father said, "My daughter speaks some Apache—learned it from our maid—but I'm not sure she understood what you said to him. Something about family." There was a note of suspicion in his deep voice. He stuck his head forward bullishly. "You kin to that killer?"

I had been, and in a way I still was, but it was too difficult to explain.

"Not since he left me to the bluecoats," was all I could say.

One afternoon, when the post was so silent that I could hear the woodpeckers hack out tiny chips of trees, the guards returned. One stood back while the other opened my cell door, but neither carried chains or pointed his weapon at me.

"The captain wants to talk to you," one guard said. "Don't do nothin' stupid till you hear what he was to say."

I took a few uncertain steps into the fort compound, squinting at the bright light. After a week in the cold, damp cell, I relished the brief warmth of sunshine.

The last few days had been grim. If the guards had not brought me more blankets, clean white-eyes clothes, and decent boots the day after Lizzie Riley came, I might not have survived. I was still in pain, but the knife wound was slowly healing, and sleep had taken care of my battering by the river.

CHAPTER TWENTY-FIVE

I found the captain pacing near the fort gates, slapping his thigh with a piece of yellow paper. I stood as straight as I was able. He might kill my body, but I would not let him steal my pride.

"I have received word from Captain Pratt of Carlisle Indian School," he gruffly declared. "He says that Daniel Hamilton is a 'good Indian.' He ran away from his outing farm after killing a white man, apparently in defense of an elderly lady who considers this Apache some part of her family. She persuaded the local officials to drop all charges."

He glared at me. "The physical description she gave of Hamilton seems to fit you."

I did not care about his last words. I was still revelling in his earlier message. Captain Pratt had spoken up for me? Annie had . . . Grandmother Annie had come to my defense? Cleared my name?

"Because Lizzie Riley's father has ties in Washington, and because his daughter absolutely swears that you did not abduct her but saved her life, I can't prove my case that you were carrying her to Scarred-by-a-Woman." He almost snorted. "But I know. You understand me? *I know you're just like him*. Today I have to let you go, but my men have orders to shoot to kill if they ever catch you with him again."

CHAPTER

26

I HID IN THE MOUNTAINS for nearly a month before I returned to Riley's Ridge to show my gratitude to Lizzie. It took that long to let my broken ribs knit, to gain strength in my wounded shoulder, to rid myself of the guilt I had carried for so long.

Now that I had forgiven Grandmother Annie for her shortcomings, I could forgive myself at last. Yusn knew I had done everything I could to save He-Who-Was-My-Cousin. I had not betrayed him. I had simply failed. My uncle would surely understand this if he loved me half as much as I loved him.

I took my time moving down the mountains, hunting as I walked. As soon as I shot a wild turkey, I hiked quickly toward Mr. Riley's growing town.

I found Riley's Ridge surprisingly active. A new store had just gone up and another had broken ground, and the people were enjoying some sort of white-eyes celebration. A few glanced my way uneasily, as they had in Pennsylvania, but nobody seemed to fear me.

A white cowboy told me how to reach Lizzie's father's giant house on the outskirts of town. When I knocked at the front door, Lizzie was the one who answered.

Her pretty eyes widened, but this time she did not smile. It was obvious that she did not recognize me. I was not surprised. My hair was still long but I had worn white-eyes clothes for the occasion.

"I owe you much more than a turkey," I told her, "but for right now, this is all I can offer."

At last she gave me a toothy grin. "Oh, it's you! You look so different all . . . dry and healthy."

Two years ago I would not have known what to do next, but I had learned a lot from Polly. I was not afraid to talk to this white-eyes girl. I even managed a small smile.

"Come in, but leave that dead thing on the porch!" she commanded brightly.

I did as she said. It felt odd, but good, somehow, to step inside. It was the first time I'd been in a white-eyes house since I'd left Pennsylvania. Already I could smell a baking pie.

"I like the way your house backs up against the woods, Miss Riley," I told her truthfully.

"Oh, don't be silly. Call me Lizzie," she insisted. Then she turned to face me, friendly but uncertain. "We never really were introduced. I'm not sure what to call you. The captain said your name is Daniel."

I pondered that a moment, wondered if I could ever hear that name again without remembering the heartless way I had received it.

I thought about the other names I had

been given, by those who loved me and those who didn't, and the meaning of each word. I thought about who I was and who I'd been, and who I'd hoped to be.

Finally, I proudly said to Lizzie, "My name is Solito. Solito Hamilton."

Over the next few days Lizzie introduced me many times that way. Once I dined with her family, I realized how hungry I was for company—Apache or white—and I didn't really want to spend another year by myself in the wilds. I knew I could do it, and that was enough.

There didn't seem to be any place for me on the reservation. It was just as beautiful as I remembered. The Apaches were just as destitute, the rations just as scanty, the bluecoats just as cruel.

But I had changed. I could read and write and I had learned a white man's trade. I just didn't feel at home in my old world anymore.

Still, I did not want to go back to Pennsylvania.

I had to buy paper to write to my grandmother, so I asked Lizzie's father for some work. At first he gave me nothing but stable-mucking and wood-chopping chores, which I did without complaining. But one day, I used my free time to repair an old saddle with split-leather seams. After Mr. Riley saw the quality of my work, he considered more seriously my claim that I was a harness maker by trade.

CHAPTER TWENTY-SIX

I slept in the loft of his barn for several weeks, while Mr. Riley quietly convinced his neighbors to let me repair their harnesses . . . and finally make one for him. It was slow, very slow, gaining their acceptance, and I knew that if it were not for Lizzie's father, the white-eyes would not even have let me stay in their town, let alone bring me their business. They all knew how I had first met Lizzie, and many of them still believed I was a secret ally of Scarred-by-a-Woman.

Mr. Riley was surprised that I didn't need his help, or Lizzie's, to write to my grandmother, or to read the letter she quickly wrote back. Grandmother Annie told me that the sight of the killing had shocked her, not just because I had done it with such Apache flair but because she had never seen anyone killed before. The dead body had shaken her with memories of the death of He-Who-Was-My-Grandfather. Still, she begged me to forgive her. I guess she did not know that I already had.

Grandmother Annie had gone to live with Ruth after I'd left, but if I wanted to come back, she promised to return to the farm she had shared with He-Who-Was-My-Grandfather. She had saved all the money I had earned during my outing time, and He-Who-Was-My-Grandfather had left me his harness-making tools in his will. If I did not want to return, she told me, she would send the tools and cash wherever I planned to start my own shop.

I was startled to realize that running my own business might actually be a possibility! It would be easy, in some ways, to stay right here in Riley's Ridge. But there were several reasons I thought I should leave the White Mountains. The bluecoat captain still thought I was a killer, and if I ever ran into trouble again, I was afraid it would take a great deal more than Mr. Riley's influence to save me. I still had made no contact with my birth family, and I did not believe this was an accident. Surely by now my story was common knowledge among the White Mountain Apaches, and if anyone suspected I was a lost child of a local family, he would have come forward. I still suspected that I was linked, somehow, to the frightened old man who'd come to my jail cell, but clearly he had not chosen to align himself with me.

Neither did the local Apaches. Even Lizzie's White Mountain Apache maid avoided me, and though I sometimes heard the sound of the tribal drum at night in the distance, I was never asked to join sacred gatherings, or even the social events to which some friendly Mexican and white-eyes cowboys were invited. And how I longed to go! It had been three years since I had been to a puberty ceremony, or a thank-you dance, or watched the heady performance of the crown dancers.

I had done nothing to offend the White Mountain tribe. But an Apache whose own family would not claim him was as welcome as . . . a Chiricahua who might be in league with a killer renegade. Yet Scarred-by-a-Woman had discarded me as he had discarded the rest of our people. I wondered, if we ever met again, if he would hesitate to kill me. After dodging the law for so long, Scarred-by-a-Woman knew perfectly well that the White Mountain Apaches, like the bluecoats, did not have enough information to find him when he went to ground deep in Geronimo's Chiricahua Mountains.

But I did.

CHAPTER 27

AS AUTUMN CAME with the Moon-of-Big-Harvest, I realized I had to start making winter plans. Mr. Riley was giving me more harness-repair business as his boom town grew, and no one had complained about my work. I had saved enough money to buy a rifle, a pretty claybank mare, and two cowboy shirts. I had even sent some cash to Uncle Angry, along with my very straightest handmade arrow. I didn't want to write a letter that some white-eyes would translate for him. I hoped he understood that I had a found a way to help my family by making money, but I had not forgotten everything he had taught me.

I was, very slowly, making friends. Oh, not the close kind—not like He-Who-Was-My-Cousin—but in time I became comfortable with some of the Rileys' cowboys. I taught them how to hunt, and how to look for sign. They taught me the tricks that went with herding cattle, hog-tying a calf or wrestling a wild steer to the ground. Joey, a buck-toothed cowboy about my age, took the time to show me how to wrap a rawhide string around all four legs in record time. I practiced roping and tying just to prove I could out-cowboy Joey and the other men. I even started carrying a rawhide string.

The white-eyes boys in town played baseball, too, but they never asked me to join them. Still, my hunger for the game was so great that I took to watching close by, and one day, when they were a player short, I trotted out to right field to catch a fly. When I thundered the ball home in time to block what would have been the scoring tie, the team at bat called my help "interference," but the captain of the other team joyfully claimed me. After the men saw how I could pitch and run, I was always welcome.

It was after one of those games—my first shut-out at Riley's Ridge—that I found the courage to approach Mr. Riley with the plan I had in mind. I wanted to build my own small cabin-shop. I would pay him rent—for his connections with my potential customers as well as the land—but any profits above that would always be mine.

At first he said no. He thought I was joking, or crazy, or both. But once he realized that I did such good work that his growing town would suffer if I left the area before another harness maker came, he agreed to my plan. I thought the rent he decided to charge me for my patch of ground was way too high, but I didn't care as long as the shop—one rough-hewn room pressed against the pine-drenched mountains—would always be mine.

I started building the place with dried saguaro ribs and old planks of wood that Mr. Riley had used and discarded. One night I carefully carved the words, "Solito Hamilton, Harness Maker," onto a long board I cut in the shape of a sign. I wrote to Grandmother Annie requesting my tools, and she sent them by train to Arizona. It took several days for Joey and me to ride north to collect them from the nearest depot in Mr. Riley's wagon, but it was worth it when I moved them into my barely finished building. I hadn't even signed a contract yet, but I was so proud!

The next day I decided to put up my sign. It was a clear day, bright but very cold, and I wore a buckskin shirt over my white-eyes clothes.

I was just about to drive in the first nail when I heard a ruckus coming from the other end of town. I turned around and spotted Joey wildly spurring his black pony toward me.

"Solito! Come quick!" he hollered as I dropped my hammer. "Mr. Riley needs you right away!"

"What's wrong?"

"It's that outlaw. The one you know! Mr. Riley says he just struck a family near the fort again. This time he swears that killer won't get away."

It took me all that night and the better part of the next day to ride to the place where Lizzie's

Apache maid had told me to look for "two trees growing straight up by the rock-topped mountain." The sun was shining brightly, but the wind was brisk. The children fled into their wickiups as they saw me coming, screaming about ghosts. Looking at their terrified small faces, I had no doubt about how much I must resemble the Apache boy Scarred-by-a-Woman had killed.

Surely he and I must hail from the same clan.

I did not dismount outside the frightened old man's wickiup. It would not be courteous to approach the home uninvited, even as a friend, let alone as an unwelcome stranger. He would come out to see me when he was ready.

Surely he knew why I had come. The instant I had heard of Scarred-by-a-Woman's last raid, I had made my decision. *Somebody had to stop him.* That somebody had to be me.

But I had to know more before I confronted him. I needed to know if it was also my duty to seek revenge for the White Mountain boy he had murdered. I was sure that my look-alike must have been some kind of relative. If that were true, I could not spare his killer, just as I could never have abandoned He-Who-Was-My-Cousin.

While I waited on the mare, I was struck by the absolute destitution of this White Mountain family. They still lived in a wickiup. Their only animal was a broken-down mule. Drying venison, a woven water *tus,* and baskets full of acorns proved they still survived in the old way.

At last the old man crawled out of his home. His wrinkled face was grim. There was fear and anger in his eyes, and some other sort of grief that I assumed was for He-Who-Was-His-Son. He offered no word of welcome.

Two wizened old women trailed him out into the sun. The eldest narrowed her eyes, her dark gaze boring into me and the claybank mare. The younger one stared at me just the way the old man had the first time he'd seen me—in terror, shock, and confusion.

"I need to know," I told the man, "if the one with scars has killed my kin."

That's when I heard a strangled cry, not from the old man but from the ancient woman behind him. Wildly she waved her scrawny arms, as though to ward off some savage beast bent on ripping out her throat.

I did not move. The middle-aged woman quickly bent down to the ground, trying to soothe the writhing older one. The old man rushed to stand before her, as though to block an impending enemy attack.

Then a girl, about five years older than I was, bolted out of the wickiup. Her eyes met mine and held. She did not look afraid, like the others, but neither did she welcome me.

But she knew. I could see it her face. *She knew me.*

"Please," I said, to her and to no one else. "I don't want to cause any trouble. I just want to know who I am."

Her mouth moved, as though she were about to speak, but no words came out before the old shrunken woman issued what could have been a death cry and collapsed.

"Witch!" She moaned. "That witch is trying to kill me!"

I had not even dismounted. I knew I should leave, but I'd been through too much to tolerate such accusations. "I am no witch!" I insisted. "I'm not here to hurt anyone!"

The old man studied the ground. The girl who was near my age slowly shook her head.

To her alone I said, "Can't you see? I was lost near here as a baby! I look just like a member of your family. I *must* belong to someone in this clan."

The old woman screamed again before the girl could answer.

The old man all but choked with rage. "Go now! Can't you see my old mother is dying? You say you mean no harm, but look what you have done to her!"

My heart twisted up inside, so tight and pained I could hardly budge. There would be no welcome here, just as I had always feared.

I looked once more at the girl, mutely pleading for her help. She did not speak to me. She did not meet my eyes.

Finally, crushing back my sorrow, I kneed the claybank and turned away.

The mare loped off at a stately pace while I held my head up high. *I was Solito Hamilton, harness maker.* The white-eyes world had not killed me. I had survived on my own as an Apache. I would find a way to make my world whole no matter what anybody did to me!

I had ridden less than an angry mile when I heard hoofbeats behind me. Tensely I turned.

It was not the bluecoats. It was not Scarred-by-a-Woman. It was the girl.

CHAPTER 28

INSTANTLY I TURNED back my horse to meet her.

"You know me!" I called out as I faced her. "You know who my people are."

Her eyes brimmed with tears as she pulled up her raggedy mule. "I can prove nothing, but in my heart, I know."

I took a deep breath and waited.

"You look just like He-Who-Was-My-Brother, except you are older. You are the age he would be now." She lowered her voice, because it was never wise to speak of the dead. Softly she added, "He was a fine boy. You would have been proud of him."

I wasn't sure what to say. Just once, I wanted someone to be proud of *me*.

"I was five years older than He-Who-Was-My-Brother, and I remember quite clearly the night he was born. My grandmother was there, of course, and my father waited with the men.

"My mother was still quite young. She has always been a gentle person. My father's mother was—is—very strong. She despises the blue-coats above all things. She hates the way they try to change us, the way they scoff at our sacred rituals."

I nodded once.

"She believes in the old ways with every part of her heart. She would never do wrong in the eyes of Yusn."

I felt a queasiness in my stomach, a feeling I could not trust. I had come for a simple answer. This girl seemed to have an explanation, but it was *not* a simple one.

"My mother had a very bad time giving birth to He-Who-Was-My-Brother. I heard her scream for what seemed like days. Finally I heard the baby cry, too, and I knew the worst was over. My grandmother called me in to take the baby, to hold him while she tried to give my mother ease." The girl's voice broke, and as she cried, her words became hard to follow. "She wanted to do what was right for an Apache mother-in-law. Do you understand?"

"I understand that she wanted to do what was right," I answered slowly. "I don't understand what she did that you must think was wrong."

Tears now rivered down her face. "When I went in to see my mother, she was asleep—the kind of sleep that lasts for a very long time. I was afraid she was dead or dying. I had never been so frightened in my life."

Again her eyes begged me for some kind of forgiveness. "I was only five."

Still, I waited. She had spoken only of the

birth of her brother. What did this have to do with me?

"I had put the baby in his new cradleboard and tried to give him to my grandmother. But she had something in her hands, the mess from the birthing, I thought, and told me to put the baby by my mother and stay there until she returned. I put the baby down and turned to my mother, trying to snuggle up to her side."

The sickness in my stomach grew unbearable.

"I had been up all night, sick and scared for my mother, and I started to fall asleep beside her. I was half-asleep, or maybe dreaming, when I heard a baby cry."

For the first time she leaned toward me and laid one quiet hand on my arm, as though she shared a secret. "The noise came from the side of the wickiup where I had left the baby, but it seemed too soft, too far away. When I woke up, I asked Grandmother if she had taken the baby to show my father. She asked me why. I told her what I had heard and that I wondered why the baby seemed to be right where I left him, when I was certain I had heard him outside."

"And she said?" I whispered.

"She said I wasn't old enough to know how loud or soft a baby cried. When I tried to tell her that I was certain the baby had not been inside the wickiup, she told me that I was rude and disrespectful to question her, and if I persisted she could tell my father I was a very bad child. I hung my head and prayed for days that she would not tell him. I loved him so much, and I had never done anything to displease him."

Her voice faded off, and for a moment, there was utter stillness in the pines.

"I was so young!" she finally whispered. "I had to believe that my grandmother was right and I had only dreamed the sound." Red danced on her angular cheeks. "It was not until years later, when I was a young girl, that I learned of the evil that can befall a family when two babies come at the same time. It is the father's mother's job to take care of her family. My grandmother only did what any good Apache mother-in-law would do."

I stared at her blankly, numbly, for so long that she finally slid off the mule and touched my shoulder to be sure I was still listening. It was hard to think when I felt as though some bluecoat had shoved my head under icy water.

But I could not hide from the truth. I looked like this girl's brother because I had been born of the same parents, of the same flesh and blood, at the very same time! We were twins like the Quaker girls I had marveled at in Pennsylvania. They had been born together, been partners, two halves of a whole all of their lives.

But I had always been empty, not quite full. I had always been one half of a twinship, always missing my identical brother. He had been born to this family, cherished and honored and brought up in the White Mountain Apache way. But I, surely the second twin, had been discarded like a broken *tus* or a piece of bad meat, cast off by the ancient one who had called me a witch.

She-Who-Was-My-Adopted-Mother should have named me Little-Left-to-Die.

CHAPTER 29

THE FIRST SNOW FELL before I came upon Scarred-by-a-Woman's tracks deep in the Chiricahua Mountains. For almost two months I had been searching for some sign of him in every cave and canyon that I had ever visited with him or my uncle. My mare had long since broken down and I was on foot now, once more counting on my hunting skills to stay alive.

Despite my constant awareness that Scarred-by-a-Woman could easily find me before I found him, it was a joy to be back in the land Yusn had made for my forefathers. What majestic stone cliffs stood guard here! As I settled in among the piñon pines and peeling red-bark trees, I knew that the white-eyes could never kill the very soul of the Chiricahua people. Yusn's high rocky land still thrived in mystery, and I desperately hoped that since I had found my way back home against all odds, someday the rest of my people would find a way to do it, too.

I knew Lizzie would be worried about me. Her father might think I had forgotten our business agreement and taken off for good. Grandmother Annie would be preparing for Christmas now. She would be wondering why I had not written to say that I'd received the tools.

My newfound sister would be waiting, too, afraid her news had led me to my death at the hands of the Evil One. I was eager to spend more time with her after I had completed this manhunt that honor forced me to pursue.

We had talked a long time in the sunshine, my sister and I, the day I had finally learned the truth about my birth. She wanted to know all about my life, and I wanted to know about hers. I had never met her before, and yet at once I felt close to her—as close as I'd once felt to Makes-a-Good-Home.

It had taken me some time to recover from the shocking sense of betrayal. But I had learned a lot about forgiveness, and, in a way, I understood what my grandmother had done. Still, I did not imagine that she would ever be reconciled to my presence, and in truth I did not want to have anything to do with her.

My sister thought I might have hope of making peace with my mother and father, though, once they recovered from the shock. After all, neither of them had ever known about me, and it took two living babies to break the twin taboo. Now I was the only one.

One afternoon when I was on the way back to my winter wickiup, I sensed a sudden stillness in the trees and knew I was not alone. I flattened myself against a giant ponderosa and waited. Nothing happened. Gradually, the jays resumed their chatter. I took a step out and cautiously moved along the trail, wondering if I had imagined my brother-creatures' warning.

But I was haunted by the sense of danger. I had wondered how long I could trail Scarred-by-a-Woman before he spotted me. He was three years older than I was—seasoned and strong—and he'd been honing his fighting skills while I'd been learning to mend harnesses and read. In pure Apache survival, I knew he had the advantage over me.

But I had some advantages that he did not have. I was fighting for love of friends and family. He was only fighting for hate. I had a future in mind, a good one, where I wouldn't have to choose between being true to my tribe or whitemanized—I could just be myself. He had no future, only living from one murder to the next. I cherished the past, as I had been taught, but I had found a way to live in the future. He was a warped distortion of the true Apache Way. Nothing could save him from himself.

I sensed the arrow just a second before it zipped past. I dropped flat and scrambled behind the nearest boulder. Another arrow struck the ground just inches from my face.

"Traitor! Coward! Did you really think you could ever conquer me?" he taunted.

I inched back without a sound, barely

dodging another arrow. I didn't have enough room to draw my bow. I didn't have my rifle.

"I knew you would track me for the bluecoats! But you have failed, Little-Left-Behind. As always."

I felt a strange stirring within me. Anger, yes, but no shame this time. Scarred-by-a-Woman had found it easy to humiliate the boy I'd once been. He would find it much harder to quell the man I had become.

"I have not failed, and I have not betrayed you to the bluecoats," I called out defiantly. "You turned against our own people. It is my duty to bring you in."

"*Our* own people?" he scoffed. "The White Mountain Apaches who live on the reservation like white-eyes sheep?"

"They are still Apache! They still have souls!" I thundered at him. "And one of them was He-Who-Was-My-Brother."

He did not hesitate for an instant. "I wondered how it was that there seemed to be two of you."

"You stole my sister out of her own home!" I accused. "For these crimes against your people, and for all the others, I must bring you to your knees."

Three years ago he would have laughed. Even three months back. But now, as I stood bravely, Scarred-by-a-Woman looked at my face and saw something he did not expect to find. He was looking for a boy called Little-Left-Behind.

Instead he saw a man who had just found his family . . . and made his own place.

Suddenly he rushed at me, in a long bounding leap that should have dropped him right on top of me and pinned me to the ground. Another Apache would have pulled out his knife, run to attack him, met his blade with the clang of metal. I knew that's what he was expecting me to do.

It was what Uncle Angry had taught me.

But this time I heard another voice inside me, *my* voice, a voice that said I could only outwit Scarred-by-a-Woman if I took him by surprise. I had to do something he would never expect.

I would fight like a white-eyes.

Instinctively, I pretended he was covering second base. As he flew toward me, I raced toward a sandy patch behind him and slid just to his left on my right leg. He came down hard, baffled, on his stomach, while I rolled up on my left foot the way I had been taught at Carlisle. I whipped around before he even guessed where to look for me, pinned him to the ground, and twirled my piece of rawhide around his wrists and ankles.

Child-of-the-Water had made his fourth raid.

I took Scarred-by-a-Woman back to my father and left him without a word. It was something that had to be done, but I took no joy in it. I didn't want to be there when the White

Mountain warriors killed him. After all, he had once saved my life. Once he died, I would be the last free Chiricahua, the last warrior of our tribe.

My sister wept with gratitude. My father apologized for sending me away. I did not see the grandmother who had tried to kill me, but my birth mother poked her head out of the wickiup and came outside. She did not speak to me, but her eyes were dark with baffled grief. She walked slowly to the old mule my sister had ridden the day we'd met and led him toward me.

I knew my White Mountain family had almost nothing, but giving gifts was the Apache way. It would be rude to refuse the pathetic mule, so I thanked her as I took the buckskin lead. I would return soon with a gift of my own. Someday, my birth family might yet acknowledge me.

I rode the mule back to Riley's Ridge, hoping I had not lost my opportunity to start up my harness-making business there. I had left abruptly, before I'd even had a chance to nail up my new shop sign. By now I wouldn't be surprised if Mr. Riley had reclaimed the wood or rented my tiny cabin to somebody else. After all, he was a white-eyes.

It was shortly before sundown when I reached the town, so snugly pressed against the majestic White Mountains of my birth. The aspen leaves still trembled. The pines still sparkled in the golden light. The white-eyes might think they had claimed this wild country, but I knew Arizona was still Yusn's holy place.

As the weary mule jogged through busy Main Street, I slowly realized that no one in Riley's Ridge seemed to be averting their eyes from me.

"We've missed you at the ranch!" yelled Joey, my cowboy friend.

I heard somebody whisper, "There's the brave man who saved us from the killer!"

A teammate called, "Hey, Hamilton, glad you're back! We need you to pitch next spring if we're going to win!"

I greeted them all with a quiet, from-the-soul smile as I rode proudly to the little cabin I had built with my own hands. It was still there, still full of harness-making tools, still waiting for me to start my new life.

By the hitching-post, someone had hung my hand-carved sign:

Solito Hamilton, Harness maker.

Proof that I was finally home.

A NOTE FROM THE AUTHOR

ALTHOUGH SOLITO and his family members are fictional characters, the story of the Chiricahua Apaches' removal from Arizona is true. Captain Pratt, General Miles, and Chief Naiche were real people who behaved much as they do in *The Last Warrior*. Geronimo is also a genuine historical figure, but his story is often clouded by myth and legend. To this day, Apaches are divided in their view of him. Some see him as a hero; others regard him as a trouble-maker or villain.

The U.S. Government never kept any of its promises to Chiricahuas, who remained prisoners-of-war in Florida, Alabama, and Oklahoma for twenty-seven years. During this time, countless Apaches died of starvation and disease. In 1913, most of the survivors joined the Mescalero Apaches on their reservation in New Mexico. Some farmed individual plots in Oklahoma. As a tribe, the Chiricahuas were never again allowed to live in their Arizona mountain stronghold.

I am indebted to Eve Ball (author of

Indeh: An Apache Odyssey) for her faithful recording of the personal narratives of many Apaches who lived during the early reservation period. The tribe's present-day descendants eloquently recount this painful chapter of their heritage in the PBS Home Video, *Geronimo and the Apache Resistance.* Every American should see it.

I am also grateful to the following authors for their personal narratives and/or research: Jason Betzinez, Angie Debo, Geronimo (as told to S. M. Barrett and Asa Daklugie), Grenville Goodwin, James L. Haley, Thomas E. Mails, Morris E. Opler, and H. Henrietta Stockel. The staffs of the Cumberland County Historical Society, St. Augustine Historical Society, White Mountain Apache Culture Center, Helen P. Wright Library, and The Crown Dancer (an Indian crafts shop in Pinetop, Arizona) graciously helped me track down hard-to-find information. Many Apaches and non-Apaches, both on and off the reservation, kindly took the time to answer my many questions. Thanks to you all.

ABOUT THE AUTHOR

SUZANNE PIERSON ELLISON'S academic background in English and Ethnic Studies, as well as sixteen years as a bilingual teacher (Spanish/English), prepared her well to write historical fiction from the eyes of a person whose culture is very different from her own. She was moved to write *The Last Warrior* following a trip to the beautiful White Mountain Apache Reservation, where she was struck by the great contrast between the tales of the old-timers and the lives of modern Apache teenagers.

Suzanne's motivation to tell the story of Solito also stemmed from her response to "the countless Native American memories of horrific off-reservation-school experiences and the continuing stretch non-white cultural groups must make to bridge two different worlds." Suzanne is a middle-school teacher and has published twenty-two novels that emphasize accurate history, especially that of minorities, whose stories so often go untold.

When Suzanne made a change from teaching elementary to middle school, she became intimately involved with the literature of that age and focused on helping her students develop their love of reading. Her students were a valuable test audience in the development of this book.

Along with American history, Suzanne's many interests include quilting, music, Native American culture, and the Dodgers. She lives in Ventura, California, with her husband, Scott, teenaged daughter Tara, and three beloved cats.